CHOICES

CHOICES

ELAINE SCOTT

MORROW JUNIOR BOOKS / NEW YORK

Printed in the United States of America.
1 2 3 4 5 6 7 8 9 10

Library of Congress Cataloging-in-Publication Data

Scott, Elaine, 1940–
Choices.

Summary: After football fever causes seventeen-
year-old Beth to become an unwitting participant in
the vandalism of a rival high school, her fight for
her civil rights brings her both disillusionment and
a recognition of new loyalties.
[1. School vandalism—Fiction.   2. Civil rights—
Fiction.   3. High schools—Fiction.   4. Schools—
Fiction]   I. Title.
PZ7.S419Ch   1989   [Fic]   88-34537
ISBN 0-688-07230-5

※ FOR CINDY AND GREG, ※
OF COURSE

Beth O'Connor stared at the wall of toilet paper in front of her. There were dozens of packages—scented and unscented, embossed or plain—all in an array of colors rising in front of her. Eventually, she found what she was looking for—a bargain brand that offered eight rolls in basic white for $1.89. Beth placed four packages into the grocery cart and quickly wheeled it to the checkout counter where her friend, Carl Loessing, was cashier.

"Doing a little decorating, huh?" Carl said as he slid the packages over the scanner.

"Yep," Beth answered. "Martha and I have to do Jed's house tonight. I hope this is enough paper."

Carl's eyes scanned the packages. "Thirty-two rolls.

It oughta be plenty," he said as he totaled up the bill. "We're gonna make Woodrow eat the Astroturf before it's over."

Carl and Beth smiled at each other in anticipation of this Saturday night's football game between Millington High School and its traditional rival, Woodrow Wilson High. Already, the game had gotten plenty of media attention, with sportswriters from as far away as Houston and Dallas calling both coaches to get quotes and bits of inside information.

The mayor of Fort Preston was delighted that his medium-sized east Texas town had not one but two high schools that could field championship-caliber teams. He had even declared this next Saturday "High School Football Day." Everyone who knew anything about football agreed that the team that won Saturday night would go on to become the state champion. The only competition was a team from El Paso, and experts felt that either Millington or Woodrow could whip them handily.

Beth offered Carl a ten-dollar bill. After he counted out the change he looked around the store, then leaned forward to speak conspiratorially.

"I'm getting some of the peppers free. A new produce order comes in the morning, and we won't be able to sell the peppers that are left in the store tonight. Mr. Steinmacher says I can have them—he remembers when his kids went to Millington. Anyway, there're two unopened cartons in the back. That's a bunch of free ammunition. It'll be great."

Carl laughed in a way that made a small shiver go

through Beth. The tomato and pepper war—a battle that the senior boys of each school undertook every year—had been discouraged by the faculties of both Millington and Woodrow. Nevertheless, each year on the morning of the game between the two schools, students from Millington could count on arriving at school to find their campus strewn with bits of smashed tomatoes, and students at Woodrow were equally certain to find green peppers littering theirs. Rotten tomatoes and peppers turned up in unlikely places at both schools—and in more than a few football players' lockers.

"Just be careful what you do with those peppers," Beth said. "Remember, Clara Cougar needs her partner for the game."

Clara and Casius Cougar were Millington High School's student mascots—a privilege that was bestowed on two seniors each year by vote of the student body.

"Never fear, Clara dear. I've never let you down yet, have I?" Carl was shoving the packages of toilet paper into grocery bags as he talked.

"Except for the time you couldn't find your cougar head. I thought I was going to have to lead the team onto the field by myself." Despite the serious tone she tried to take, Beth couldn't help smiling at the memory of tall, slender Carl, dressed as Casius Cougar, frantically searching for the rest of his costume. Jed Stuart, the team's quarterback, produced the papier-mâché cougar head just before Carl's face turned as red as his hair. Carl's short temper was legendary around Millington, and the excitement of seeing him "go off" often caused members of the football team to play practical jokes on him.

Beth looked at her watch. "I've gotta get going or Martha and I won't get anything done. See you at school tomorrow," she said over her shoulder as she left the store.

Outside, Beth shivered as she wheeled the grocery cart across the parking lot toward her mother's car. A cold front—a "Norther," the Texans would call it—had blown in from Canada earlier in the day, its gusting winds and driving rains pushing the last of summer's hot, muggy weather out into the Gulf of Mexico. Although it was practically the end of October, fall was just now making an appearance. A time and temperature sign across the street flashed. It was 6:30 in the evening, and 43 degrees.

I'll have to wear a sweater tonight—a heavy one, Beth thought happily to herself as she loaded her cargo into the trunk and started for home, five minutes away. She slowed down as she turned onto Moormeadow Road and approached the decorative signs that marked the entrance to her neighborhood. The signs were actually small brick walls that curved slightly—like parentheses—on each side of the road. Large gold letters on each wall spelled out "Meadowglen." In the lower corner of the left wall two smaller signs announced that the subdivision was protected by Laughlin Security Services and that door-to-door solicitation was strictly forbidden.

Tonight, however, the wall on Beth's right had been

completely wrapped in butcher paper so that it resembled a giant package. Green letters, several feet high, proclaimed that this subdivision had been renamed "Larry's Lair." Beth slowed the car to a crawl in order to study the sign. The green lettering had been outlined in black—green and black were Millington High School's colors. It looked good—a very neat job. Although Larry was just a sophomore at Millington, he had already made the varsity football team. He was a nice kid—a neighbor who lived only two blocks away.

After giving the sign another appreciative glance, Beth hurried toward home. Fortunately, her mother was still working at the dining room table, making Halloween tray favors for the Children's Hospital. She didn't look up from her task except to call out, almost absentmindedly, "You home, Beth?"

"Sure am." Beth hurried to her bedroom with her purchases. There was no point in drawing her mother's attention to the toilet paper.

Once in her room, Beth stacked the toilet paper in a corner, setting the packages alongside the rolls of butcher paper and jars of poster paint that she and Martha had accumulated over the weekend. She drew a line through "Get T.P." on a list of things to do that lay on her desk. Then she looked at the butcher paper. Four rolls. That should be plenty. I just hope Martha remembers the brushes, she thought to herself as she snapped on the radio. A raucous voice blared into the silence of the room. "We have a Blue Norther in here tonight, folks. Get those tender plants protected—get 'em inside your garage—hear?? Old Man Winter's upon us here in Texas . . . gonna drop all the way to thirty-five degrees. Brrrrrr!!!"

Beth hugged herself appreciatively and rubbed her hands briskly over her arms. Reaching up, she took a large plastic storage box from the top shelf of her closet and turned it upside down, shaking sweaters and mothballs out onto her bed. Dressed in nothing but her bra and blue jeans, Beth sang along with the radio as she picked through her sweaters, deciding which one to wear. Suddenly her bedroom door pushed open and her younger sister, Ruthanne, landed rather than sat on the twin bed that was reserved for overnight guests.

Beth grabbed for a sweater, any sweater, to cover herself. She was conscious of the fact that she more than filled the lacy bra she wore, and she could feel the blush burning in her cheeks. "Knuckles are for knocking, Ruthie. Use yours once in a while—okay? I have no privacy around here." Beth addressed this last comment to her own reflection in the mirror.

"It's just us girls," Ruthanne said. She took a noisy bite from the apple she was eating, then wiped apple juice away from the corners of her mouth with the back of her free hand. "What are you doing, trying on outfits for tomorrow?" Ruthanne had a habit of asking a question and supplying a possible answer, all in one sentence.

"No, I'm not trying on for tomorrow," said her sister. "I'm trying on for tonight. I'm going out."

Ruthanne's mouth dropped open. "Out? Where?

You know we can't go out on school nights. Mother will kill you!" Her voice was quivering with indignation and outrage as she spoke, and every freckle seemed to stand out on her skin.

Beth turned to look at her sister. She smiled and spoke in the patient, patronizing tone she knew would infuriate the fourteen-year-old further. "No, Mother would kill *you*. You're a freshman; I'm a senior. I can go out—especially when the Millington Misses are decorating." Beth glanced at her watch. "I've got to hurry. Martha's picking me up in a few minutes." She tossed a green sweater to Ruthanne. "I've outgrown this. You can have it. It'll be good to wear for the pep rally tomorrow."

"Keep it. I don't want it," Ruthanne said, tossing it back at her sister.

"Everybody dresses in school colors for the rallies, Ruthie," Beth said. Then a sudden, incredible thought hit her, and she looked at her younger sister sharply. "You know we have a pep rally tomorrow, don't you? The Woodrow game is this Saturday night. You haven't been so busy messing with Dunney that you forgot, have you?"

"I'm not 'messing' with Dunney. I'm training him for the barrel races. And how could I forget about the game with it being blathered all over the news?"

"Well, of course it's in the news. It's a big game. Whoever wins will be the new state champion."

"Who cares?" Ruthanne said.

"Everybody does, you dummy."

Beth began to rummage in the top drawer of her

7

chest, the one that held a potpourri of notes, pencils, stickers, student council campaign buttons, class schedules from past semesters, and invitations to parties long since over. She found what she was looking for and tossed it to her sister.

"Here's a football schedule. Don't lose this one."

"I didn't lose my other one," Ruthanne said, although, in fact, she had. "And I didn't forget the game. I just don't live and breathe Millington and football, like you do."

Ruthanne picked up the folded card from the floor where it had landed and studied the picture on the front. The Millington Cougars were massed on the fifty-yard line of Burford Stadium, each member of the team wearing an appropriately fierce facial expression. In contrast, six cheerleaders wore brave and toothy smiles as they balanced in a precarious pyramid on one side of the team. Beth's friend, Martha Worley, stood on top of the pyramid. On the other side, Beth and Carl posed in the fake fur costumes of Casius and Clara Cougar.

"You and Carl should have taken off your heads. Nobody can tell who's inside," said Ruthanne.

"Everybody knows Carl and I are the mascots. We wanted the heads to stay on. It looks better for the picture," Beth answered in a deliberately agreeable, if somewhat muffled, voice, coming as it was from the interior of a green-and-black striped sweater she was pulling over her head. When it was on and adjusted, Beth checked her appearance in the mirror. Turning to Ruthanne, she said, "Do you think I should wear this one or the solid black?"

"Wear whatever you want. I don't care." Ruthanne finished her apple, chewing it down until the core was limp and brown and broken. She idly tossed the remains into Beth's wastebasket, then peered into the sacks of toilet paper by the door. "Do you have to buy all this stuff or do the Misses pay for it?"

"Not that it's any of your business, but I bought this stuff myself. The Misses have already spent their treasury for this year. The dues are only five dollars a girl."

"Yeah, well, there must be at least a hundred and fifty senior girls. That's a lot of money."

"Not everybody joins the Misses, Ruthie. Only the ones who are . . . well, active, you know."

"You mean 'popular,' so why don't you just say it?" Ruthanne asked. "Let me tell you, Mom's going to be hot when she sees all this stuff. She's started to clip coupons for groceries. Can you imagine that? Our mother, clipping coupons?"

"Well, what's the matter with that? Clipping coupons saves money," Beth said as she twisted and turned to get a view of herself in the mirror from every angle.

"That's just it. Mom's trying to save it, and here you are wasting it."

Beth spun around and looked at her sister. "I don't spend nearly as much on toilet paper as one sack of feed for that horse costs, Ruthie, and you know it."

"Well, you have Barney," Ruthanne countered, gesturing to a large black Labrador that dozed in a corner of Beth's room.

"We all have Barney," Beth corrected. "He's been here practically since I was born."

"*Anyway*," Ruthanne said in an impatient tone, "as I was saying, I heard Mother and Dad talking just yesterday. Dad said the bank has a lot of customers who aren't paying back their loans, and he's real worried. Maybe the bank will close down and he'll lose his job, like Beverly Suchin's dad did."

Beth was quiet for a moment, thinking about the people she knew who had lost jobs in the area. Most of the men worked in the oil industry, like Mr. Suchin had. Until her horse was sold, Beverly had kept it in the same stable where Ruthanne kept Dunney.

Beth peered closely at her sister. "You're worried that you're going to have to sell Dunney, aren't you? Is that what this is all about? Well, don't worry. Dad's not going to lose his job. He'll just foreclose and get the bank its money, that's all."

"He will not! You know Dad's not that mean." Ruthanne looked horrified. "All I know is, Mom told me if I want a new saddle I'll have to pay for half of it. And me with baby-sitter wages! But I still say horses make a lot more sense than those stupid silly Misses." Ruthanne flounced out of the room and her sister called after her, "You'll feel different when you're a senior."

Beth picked up her brush and ran it through her short, dark hair, then pumped two squirts of her treasured Lauren cologne behind each ear. She was ready to go. Quietly, she made several trips between her room and the entrance hall, carefully stacking the toilet paper and poster paint by the front door. She was carrying out the last of the butcher paper when two short blasts from a car horn sounded outside.

10

"That's Martha, Mother. I'm going now," Beth called toward the dining room, hoping that her mother would be satisfied with a shouted "good-bye" of her own.

"Wait a minute, Bethany, I want to talk to you." Beth heard the sound of a chair scraped hastily across the floor, and Joanne O'Connor quickly appeared in the entrance hall, holding a half-completed witch in one hand. With her free hand, she tucked a wisp of hair back into her French twist. Mrs. O'Connor looked elegant in her beige gabardine skirt, red cotton polo shirt, and red canvas espadrilles. Beth could not remember a time when her mother had not been completely, and appropriately, dressed for whatever activity she was pursuing, including working in the yard.

"Honestly, Bethany, I don't understand all this," her mother began, gesturing to the bulging sacks of toilet paper, paint, and butcher paper that stood by the front door. She glanced at her watch and went on, "It's already a little past seven, and from the looks of all these supplies, you've got hours of work ahead of you. Why in the world you girls spend your money to buy toilet paper, of all things, to litter up these football players' houses before every single game is simply beyond me. It's . . . why, it's just plain tacky, that's what it is." Joanne O'Connor had been raised in Louisiana, and "tacky" was one of her favorite adjectives.

Beth drew in a deep breath and met her mother's gaze with a steady smile. They had had this discussion before. "I've told you, it's not littering, Mother. We clean it up afterward. And anyway, we do it with permission—the school's and the guy's parents'. It's fun. It builds spirit for the games." As if to clinch the argument, Beth added, "The parents love it. It's an honor to have the Millington Misses T.P. your house before a game. Then everyone knows you're the parent of a varsity football player."

Two more toots, this time insistent, came from the car at the curb. With a resigned sigh, Joanne O'Connor opened the door for Beth and waved her hand at the girl behind the wheel, who smiled and waved a hello in return. Then Mrs. O'Connor raised a forefinger in a "wait a minute" gesture and Martha nodded in response. Turning to Beth, she said, "I seem to remember some trouble last year. Wasn't somebody hurt over in Kingwood doing this sort of foolishness?"

"Oh, that," Beth said dismissively. "One of their girls fell out of a tree and broke her arm or something, I'm not sure. It was an accident . . . it could have happened any time. I could break my leg if I fell over Barney in the middle of the night. Accidents happen." Beth was transferring the bags of toilet paper from the entrance hall to the front porch as she talked. Her mother leaned against the frame of the open door, twirling the tiny witch between her thumb and forefinger.

"Well, I can't be the only parent who feels this way. Maybe I should ask some of the others. Maybe we should get together and do something. . . ." Her voice trailed off at the end of the sentence, and she pushed the wayward lock of hair back into place once again.

12

Something twisted inside Beth. Adrenaline poured into her system, and although the night air felt cool to her cheeks, her palms began to sweat. While her mother's comments seemed casual enough, Beth knew that Joanne O'Connor was not a woman to be taken lightly when she had a cause to champion. She looked at her mother and drew in an unsteady breath.

"Mother, promise me you won't do, or say, anything—please. It's fun, and it doesn't hurt a thing. Everybody counts the days until they're a senior and can join the Millington Misses, so they can decorate for football season. All the schools around here have done it for years—you know that. Don't ruin it for us. Please."

Beth was breathing hard. If her mother managed to stop the Millington Misses, no one would speak to Beth. They would never, ever, in a million years, forgive her. In her mind's eye she could already see the balance of her senior year stretching in front of her, friendless—and endless.

Mrs. O'Connor leaned forward to give her daughter a perfunctory kiss on the cheek. "Get home as soon as you can, and tell Martha to drive carefully."

"Promise me you won't say anything."

"Who would I say it to? It seems everyone in charge supports it—legalized littering. But while you're out tonight, you and Martha might consider decorating the yard of just one honor student."

Relief flooded through Beth. She smiled at her mother and pursed her lips in a pantomime of a kiss. "I'll be home by midnight. I promise," she said. As she ran down the rest of the walk toward the open tailgate of the station wagon, she sent a silent prayer upward. "Please, God, don't let her find out the Misses are decorating bedrooms tonight."

Martha was struggling with a long aluminum extension ladder, trying to move it over to make room for Beth's supplies. When she straightened up, she looked at her friend and said, "What took you so long? I thought you'd never get away. You and your mom having a fight?" She slammed the tailgate shut as she talked.

"Not a fight, just a discussion. She thinks we should decorate honor students' houses. Can you imagine? But I don't want to push my luck with her, so I have to be home by midnight at the latest—okay?"

Martha glanced at the digital clock on the car's dashboard. The phosphorescent green numbers blinked 7:13. "We'll make it. We've got plenty of time," she said as she turned the key in the ignition. Immediately the car filled with music from the girls' favorite country and western radio station. Willie Nelson was just finishing a song about Luckenbach, Texas.

Martha pressed two buttons, and the windows on either side of the front seat lowered with a soft whirring sound. "You don't mind if we open the windows, do you?" she asked. "It's real football weather now."

"That it is. That it is," Beth answered, as she poked her head out of the window to draw in deep lungfuls of the cool pine-scented air. It felt as if she were inhaling happiness. The moon hung in the sky, full and bright, so bright that it made the bits of mica in the concrete street sparkle like diamonds. Thoughts of the worrisome conversation with her mother faded, and Beth gave way to the joy of being seventeen and out for an evening's adventure with her best friend. "Oh, I love a rainy night, I love a rainy night . . ." she sang along with Martha and the car radio, laughing to herself at the incongruity of those lyrics for a night like this. The station wagon slowly twisted its way through the darkened neighborhood toward its destination in another neighborhood a mile and a half away.

CHAPTER

TWO

"Toss me another roll, will you?" For the past ten minutes Beth had been invisible, completely concealed by the branches of a giant oak tree, one of at least a dozen that grew in the Stuarts' front yard. Thousands of oak and pine trees dotted the neighborhoods in this part of Fort Preston. They gave relief to the unrelenting flatness of the land and increased the value of the homes that were built here.

The branches shook as Beth climbed down from her perch high in the tree. She balanced herself at a midway point on the extension ladder, curled one arm around the tree trunk for support, and stretched her other arm downward, her hand open and ready, anticipating the catch.

Martha, down on all fours on the walkway fifteen feet below, was lettering a butcher-paper banner with the words "Millington's Menace—Jed Stuart #59." Without looking up she said, "I'm working, too, you know. I ought to make you come down and get it yourself."

"C'mon, toss it to me," Beth wheedled. "I've been up and down this ladder at least forty times. My legs feel like cooked spaghetti—they won't make one more climb. This is the last tree. Just a few more swags and I'm through."

Martha stopped painting long enough to pull the last roll of toilet paper from the bag and toss it up to Beth, who caught it and pinned it under her arm. Then she gingerly turned herself around on the ladder until she faced the tree limb that was her target. It jutted out from the trunk at the level of her thigh and then, after a few feet of horizontal growth, bent slightly downward. She studied the branch, deciding whether she should risk decorating it or not. It looked passably sturdy near the trunk of the tree, but she couldn't tell much about it after it began its downward slope. Beth had an eye for this sort of thing, and she felt the limb really needed to be decorated if this tree, the largest one in Jed's yard, was to have any kind of symmetry.

Tensing every muscle, as if that effort would some-how make her lighter, she slowly lowered herself onto the limb, until she was straddling it. Strands of toilet paper and airy wisps of Spanish moss hung from the branches above and around her; they brushed against her face and fluttered in her eyes. Irritated, she pushed them away, and was surprised to find a fine film of sweat coating her forehead. Small, twiglike branches picked at her sweater and pulled at her jeans as she tentatively inched her way along until the limb thinned to the point that it shuddered under her weight. She began to work, draping the toilet paper as carefully as she and Ruthanne draped tinsel on the Christmas tree—one strand at a time, each one centered, so that the sides hung evenly. Slowly she worked her way backward, easing herself toward safety, until once again she came to the sturdy right angle where the limb joined the trunk. Beth leaned back against the oak's fat spine, resting while her heartbeat returned to normal.

"Are you going to stay up there forever?" Martha was standing now, holding the butcher-paper sign she had painted. "Come on down and help me hang this one across the front porch. We haven't got much time, Cinderella—not if you have to be home by midnight. We've still got to do Jed's bedroom."

Beth looked at her watch. It was eleven-thirty. She was shocked at how long it had taken to drape the trees. Quickly, she climbed down the ladder, and within a few minutes the two girls had the banner in place.

Tonight was the first time the Millington Misses had ever decorated inside their football players' homes. Because the upcoming game was so important, a group of parents in the Millington Booster Club had decided that the boys might enjoy the surprise and extra "boost" of finding not only their yards but also their bedrooms decorated. The boys' parents had agreed to get their football players out of the house while the Misses did their work, and Martha had been in charge of making the arrangements for this evening with Mr. and Mrs. Stuart.

"Do you have a key to the house?" Beth asked as she and Martha approached the Stuarts' front door.

Martha shook her head. "Adelaide told me where she hides the extra one. Wait here. I'll be back with it in a minute." Martha disappeared around the side of the house and quickly returned carrying a key on a University of Texas key ring.

Curious, Beth couldn't resist asking, "Where'd she have it?"

"I'll never tell," Martha answered with a smile. "You get the stuff while I open the door."

French double doors led into the Stuarts' entrance hall. It was a large welcoming space. The living room opened to the right of it; the dining room to the left. A winding stairway rose in front of the girls, and beneath its curve, against the back wall, stood a small mahogany chest. On top of it there was a note, which Martha read aloud.

"Girls, there are Cokes in the fridge, and fudge, too, if you aren't watching your figures! We'll try to keep Jed out until a little past midnight, so you can do your 'thing' undisturbed. It's really so sweet of the Misses to go to all this trouble for our boys . . ." The note was signed Adelaide and Jed Sr. It was written on notepaper that had black hoofprints all around its edges and "Millington Parents' Booster Club" written in green block letters across the top.

"Isn't that sweet of Adelaide?" Martha said, folding

the note and putting it in her purse. Then she headed for the kitchen as naturally as if she were in her own home. As she went, she looked over her shoulder at Beth and said, "You want a Coke or something?"

Beth shook her head, although, in truth, she was thirsty. She didn't feel comfortable being in someone's home when the owners weren't there—even if she and Martha did have permission. Beth wondered if Martha was feeling the same way, but thought better of asking her—she'd just call her a "wuss" again. It was Martha's very own word, applied sparingly so it wouldn't lose its effect. Beth remembered the first time Martha had used it on her. It came out like a curse, the *s*'s in the word hissing like a snake before it strikes as they echoed across the parking lot of the Mauzy Chevrolet dealership. That was three years ago, during the freshman girls' volleyball team initiation. As part of the ceremonies, the seniors had insisted that the freshman girls grease their buttocks with Vaseline and leave their bottom prints on the plate glass windows of the showroom. Beth could not bring herself to do it—it was just too embarrassing.

"You are such a WUSS-S-S-S-S!!" Martha had said, loudly and with venom, as she zipped her jeans and wiped the Vaseline off her hands with a towel that the captain of the team handed her. The captain laughed at Martha's comment, and the seniors had taken up the chant—"WUSS, WUSS, WUSS"—only stopping when the flashlight of the night watchman darted across the showroom like a laser. The girls fled the scene, and Beth had nursed a resentment against

Martha for days, until Martha finally kidded her out of it. She didn't want to be called a wuss again; she wasn't going to say anything about being uncomfortable in Jed's house.

Beth's thoughts were interrupted as Martha returned to the entrance hall carrying two Cokes and a paper towel full of fudge. "Here. Try some," she said, offering the chocolate mountain to Beth. "We'll just hurt Adelaide's feelings if we don't eat it."

Beth took the offered Coke, but virtuously turned down the fudge. Then she and Martha climbed the stairs to the second floor of the Stuart home.

The long upstairs hallway had been turned into a Hall of Fame featuring the Stuart children. To Beth's left hung photographs of Tiffany Stuart, who was a year older than Ruthanne. She played tennis and rode horses. Beth recognized the neighborhood stables in one of the shots of Tiffany on horseback. It was the same stable that Ruthanne used for Dunney. Beth stopped to study the right-hand wall, which was reserved for photographs of Jed. There was Jed, the football star. His head looked tiny above enormous shoulders fleshed out by plastic forms and padding. Next, there was Jed caught in midair as he sank a basket, and finally, there he was squatting in the sand, catcher's mask lifted to reveal his face, posing for the baseball picture. Adelaide Stuart had framed and hung the team photographs, too. In each of them, she had drawn a little red circle around Jed's face. Farther down the hallway, apart from the sports gallery, eleven years of school pictures paraded by, showing

Jed progressing from a skinny little boy with spiky black hair and clear blue eyes to the handsome, self-confident young man who smiled at Beth from the junior class picture—senior pictures weren't scheduled until next spring. Jed Stuart. Class Favorite. Beth's favorite, too—and she hoped he knew that.

Martha was coaxing her down the hall, toward Jed's bedroom. Beth had never been in a boy's bedroom before, and her heart was pounding as she crossed its threshold. It was surprisingly neat—somehow, she had always thought of boys as messy creatures. The double bed was made, but one pillow had been pulled out from beneath the plain blue corduroy spread. The spread itself was rumpled, indicating that Jed had been lying on top of it before he left. Beth looked at the place where Jed's body had been, and feelings stirred inside her that made her turn her head away quickly and walk purposefully across the room to Jed's desk, where she put rolls of crepe paper, masking tape, and scissors. Her eyes fell on a photo of Jed's father that hung over the desk. It had been taken when he was sworn in as a member of the Board of Education of the Valley Stream Independent School District. Mr. Stuart was standing ramrod straight, his right hand raised to take the oath of office. Adelaide Stuart stood by his side, beaming. She was wearing a corsage of white carnations, tied with green and black ribbons.

"Is Mr. Stuart still on the school board?" Beth asked Martha as she stared at the picture.

"Oh sure. He's been reelected once; I think he's president now." Martha had walked over and was studying the photograph now. "My mother and dad were his campaign chairmen, didn't you know that?"

If Beth knew it once, she had forgotten it. The school board elections had not been topics of conversation in the O'Connor household. She glanced at the photograph one more time; then she saw a University of Texas catalogue that lay on Jed's desk. Beth glanced at the cover and said to Martha, "I can't believe it. Jed's already got the new U.T. catalogue. I didn't think it was out yet."

"That doesn't surprise me," said Martha, as she pulled a balloon to stretch it out. "If your father had been their star quarterback, and you were going there on a football scholarship, you'd get a catalogue hot off the press, too."

"I didn't know Mr. Stuart had played football either," Beth said.

Martha dropped her lower jaw and raised her eyebrows into her forehead in mock surprise. "Where have you been, girl? Jed Sr. was one of the best. He even played for St. Louis for a few seasons. But he had trouble with his ankles and had to quit." Martha put down the last of the balloons and walked across the room as she talked.

"Whoa-a-a. What have we here? Looks like our Class Favorite wears Calvin Klein briefs." Martha was holding up a pair of jeans that had been tossed over the chair in front of Jed's desk. The underwear was still inside, as if jeans and briefs had been removed in haste, as one unit.

Beth looked and saw the designer logo that was stitched into the elastic of the waist. She felt her face go crimson at the intimacy of what she was seeing, and she glared at Martha, angry without really knowing why. "Martha! Put those down! Let's get on with this and get out. I've got to get home."

Martha dropped the jeans as if they were a match about to burn her fingers. "Well, well, well," she said. "No need to be touchy. Help me twist this crepe paper together; we'll have it up in no time." She was unrolling lengths of green and black streamers, and she handed one end of them to Beth, who stood silently while Martha twisted, then taped the streamers in one corner of the ceiling. "You like Jed, don't you?" Martha said, getting down off the chair and indicating that Beth should tape her end in the opposite corner.

"Of course I like Jed, don't you?"

"Yeah, but not like you do. It's written all over you whenever you look at him. But take my advice and forget it. I've known him since kindergarten. Jed's too stuck on Jed to do anything more than play the field."

"I didn't ask for your advice, thank you."

"Suit yourself," Martha said cheerfully. "Don't say I didn't warn you."

The girls worked quickly, and within ten minutes, scallops of crepe paper swooped across the ceiling and green and black balloons bobbed over the headboard of the bed. Martha had made a giant card that said, "Sock it to 'em, Super Stud, with love from your Misses, Martha and Beth." She propped it against Jed's pillow.

Beth surveyed the room with satisfaction. "I think that does it," she said. "Now I've really got to get going."

"Just one more thing," said Martha, digging into her purse to find her lipstick. When she found it, she gave her lips two coats of "Revolutionary Red" and disappeared into the bathroom that connected to Jed's bedroom.

Curious, Beth followed. "Oh, Martha, no! That's such a mess to clean up, and besides, I don't like the way it looks."

"Too late now, Sweetie, it's done."

Martha had left a border of perfect lip prints around the bathroom mirror.

The girls hurried out of the house and locked it, and Martha returned the key to its hiding place. But before they climbed into the car to leave, they stepped into the middle of the street to get a better perspective on their evening's work. It was quite cold now, and they wrapped their arms across their chests to ward off the chill that came through their sweaters. Somehow, the full moon and the cold, clear night helped transform the Stuarts' yard into a surreal landscape, something of a cross between a horror movie and Disneyland. The trees, their natural shapes hidden beneath miles of toilet paper trimming, seemed to move in the evening breeze like giant ghosts dancing a bizarre hula. The butcher-paper banner, dripping rivulets of green and black poster paint, hung like a starched sheet from the roofline of the Stuarts' front porch.

"Doesn't it look great?" Martha said. "I know it's the best-decorated house in the whole school district. You did a great job with that toilet paper."

"Thanks. I think it looks pretty good, myself." Beth turned and smiled at her friend. "Your banner isn't bad, either."

"I know," Martha said matter-of-factly, unlocking the car door. As she pulled onto Washington Drive, Martha said, "Keep your eyes open for cops."

Beth craned her head out the car window. "I don't see any, but why don't you just slow down a little?"

"Because you have to get home on time, remember? We don't want Joanne to get upset."

The car's clock read 12:15 when the girls pulled up in front of the O'Connor's house. The porch light was on, but the rest of the house was dark. Her parents might be asleep, and Beth hoped Barney wouldn't greet her with lusty barks.

"You're not terribly late, Cinderella. Will your parents be mad?" Martha looked concerned.

"If Barney wakes her, Mother might be, but I don't think so—not for fifteen minutes, anyway. How about your folks? Do they care that it's a school night?"

"It's my father who gives me the most trouble. Mom's pretty cool," Martha said. "Both of them know how important this is, though."

"You're lucky," Beth said, sliding out of the car. "Don't leave until I get in, and lock your doors."

When she was safely inside her house, Beth flashed the porch light on and off, then watched as Martha pulled away from the curb. Suddenly, she was aware of being very tired. The weariness was the contented kind that often comes with physical exertion and the knowledge that you have held nothing back, and the job at hand has been well done. Barney had stayed mercifully asleep, and Beth climbed into bed eagerly and slept soundly through the night.

CHAPTER

THREE

"I think it's stupid to have to go to school at seven-fifteen in the morning for a dumb pep rally," Ruthanne said, as she and Beth climbed into their father's car the following day. Beth was carrying her Clara Cougar costume.

"You don't have to go this early. It doesn't start till eight, and you can catch the bus at seven-forty-five. Why don't you ride it, like every other freshman?" Beth twisted around in the front seat to get a look at her sister, who was staring stonily—and pointedly—out the window.

Ruthanne jerked her head around, eyes flashing. "Don't start on me about the bus. You're not about to ride it."

"That's because I'm a senior."

"What's that got to do with it?"

"Everything! Freshmen ride the bus. Seniors don't. That's all there is to it."

"That's enough!" Franklin O'Connor's voice cut through the bickering in the car like a lightning bolt, shocking the girls into silence. "I've got enough on my mind without listening to you two argue all the way to school."

Beth cut her eyes to Ruthanne and gave her sister an "I told you so" look; then she opened her government book and began to look over a list of terms she thought would appear on this morning's quiz. When the car turned onto Moormeadow Road she would have missed seeing anything if Ruthanne hadn't exclaimed, "Uh oh, would you look at that?"

Beth's head shot up in time to see that Millington's rivals had been at work in her neighborhood. Bright yellow claw tracks, symbol of Woodrow's mascot, the eagle, had been sprayed down the center of the street and up one of the light poles.

"That's bordering on real vandalism," Franklin O'Connor said, as he slowed the car to get a better look.

"Well, they always spray them around Woodrow," Beth offered in a kind of defense. "We spray green cougar paws on Millington's driveway, too. The art departments even make the stencils. It doesn't hurt anything."

"Take a look at those signs," her father said, pointing to the Meadowglen entrance signs. Beth lowered the car's window to get a better look. The sign that said "Larry's Lair" had been torn in two and someone had spray-painted "Larry's lousy" across one side of it in red paint. Red and yellow were Woodrow's colors. Hunks of smashed tomato stuck to the gold lettering of both Meadowglen signs, and more tomatoes littered the ground.

"Looks like Woodrow is really playing dirty. They could have left Larry's sign alone for just one day," Beth said as the car headed toward Washington Drive.

The three O'Connors rode on in silence. Beth gave up on the government text and instead wondered what—if anything—had been done to Jed's house overnight. She hated to think of last night's work ruined before anyone except the Stuarts had a chance to admire it. As soon as her father reached the school campus Beth strained to see if the cougar paw prints on the Parents' Drive were still intact. Mrs. Fabrion, the head of Millington's art department, had worked all yesterday afternoon with a committee from the Misses, stenciling the green paw prints in a marching pattern on the drive. Beth half expected to see yellow eagle tracks obliterating them, but the cougar prints were untouched. When the car came to a stop Ruthanne bolted from the backseat like a caged animal suddenly set free, and headed for the East Building and the early-morning study hall that was held there. Beth was slower, since she had to gather up the bulky costume along with her books. She gave the heavy car door a bump with her hip to close it and poked her head through the window. "Thanks for the ride,

Dad." Then, on impulse, she added, "Are you all right?"

She was rewarded with a smile from her father. "I'm okay, honey. I've just got a rough day ahead of me, that's all. I may have to call in some bad loans." Before Beth could say anything else, Franklin O'Connor put the car in gear again and began to pull out of the circular driveway.

"Hey, O'Connor! Get the lead out and get over here." It was Martha, yelling and waving her arms. She was already dressed in the green and black cheerleader uniform, and she was pouring green food coloring into the water reservoir of the fountain that sat in the center of Millington's front lawn. Five years ago, a few members of the Parents' Booster Club had dyed the water green before the Woodrow game, and now it was a hallowed Millington tradition.

Martha poured the last of the food coloring, and the two girls hurried across the campus, passing beneath trees that dripped toilet paper. Errant pieces of it blew across the lawn and caught in the feet of the costume Beth dragged.

They reached the girls' gym, and Martha paused at the door before she went in. "Doesn't the campus look great?" she said to Beth. Then, without waiting for an answer, she added, "Just pray it doesn't rain." Martha cast an anxious glance at a sky so blue that Beth laughed and said, "I wouldn't worry about that if I were you."

"Well, you never can tell about this Texas weather—especially at this time of year. Just pray it doesn't." The fervent sound in Martha's voice made Beth look at her curiously. Both girls were hurrying toward the locker room. "Why are you so worried?" Beth asked as she flopped the heavy costume on a narrow bench that ran in front of the lockers.

Martha opened her locker, which was next to Beth's, and began scrutinizing herself in the mirror that hung inside the door. "Do you remember the rainstorm about two weeks ago, the one that hit the day after we decorated for the Valleybrook game? Remember how long it took us to pick up the mess at the Stuarts' house?"

Beth slipped out of her jeans and nodded, needing little to remind her of that steamy afternoon after the rain had turned the toilet paper into a pulpy mush that seemed to be glued to every surface—manmade or natural—in the Stuarts' yard. It had taken all afternoon, from three-thirty until seven-thirty, to clean it up. She was late for dinner, her mother was upset, and Beth had heard about the frivolous waste—both of time and money—all through the meal.

"Well, it seems that some of the Misses didn't get their yards cleaned up like they were supposed to. Doug Swanson's parents called Mr. Pugh and reported that their yard was a mess." Martha slammed her locker door shut as if to emphasize her words.

"Are you serious? Poor Doug!" Beth said as she struggled into the cougar costume.

"Isn't it awful?" Martha said sympathetically. "I'd hate to have parents like that—especially with a principal like Pugh. You know how he hates dealing with parents."

"That is very true," Beth agreed, nodding her head

in mock solemnity. "Give me a hand with this zipper, will you? It's stuck in the fur, and I can't get it to move." As Martha began to work on the stubborn zipper, Beth asked, "Why'd Pugh talk to you? Why not complain to the girls who left the mess? By the way, who were they?"

"Beth! I can't believe you'd ask me to tell on a fellow Miss." Martha's tone was deliberately self-righteous. "Pugh talked to me because I'm president of the Misses and he wanted me to do his dirty work for him. He doesn't like to talk to kids any more than he does parents. He practically has a breakdown every morning when he makes the announcements over the P.A. system! He's always clearing his throat. What a wimp." Martha gave the zipper a final tug. It pulled free of the fur and zipped up to its stop at Beth's neck.

"Thanks," Beth said, shrugging her shoulders and settling her body into the costume. "You still haven't told me what Pugh said," she prodded.

"Just 'Now, Martha, I can't be having parents unhappy with the school 'cause you girls don't clean up, hear? I don't want to hear any more complaints about messy yards, okay? Pass it along.' The bottom line is I promised that I'd be personally responsible for seeing to it that the yards get cleaned up whether it rains or not." Martha picked up her pom-poms and gave them a shake for emphasis.

"Good grief! Practically everyone is good about cleaning up. Is that all that happened?" Beth began to straighten the green bow that tied around Clara's neck.

Martha let her mouth drop open in astonishment before she spoke. "Beth, I swear! What do you mean,

'Is that all that happened?' It means that Pugh is paying attention, and we don't want teachers or principals paying attention to what the Misses do."

"Why not?" Beth asked with some exasperation. "We're not doing anything wrong. And Pugh was a coach before he was a principal . . . football's his life. Why else do you think he wears that poison-green polyester sportscoat to every pep rally?"

"I know all that. It's just that I heard some kids got suspended over at Valleybrook . . ."

"You're kidding! What'd they do?"

Martha shrugged her shoulders. "Beats me. All I know is this—the less attention the better. We need to keep everybody happy, parents included."

"I couldn't agree with you more," Beth said fervently as the two girls left the locker room. The brilliant sunshine hurt Beth's eyes, and she lifted a hand to shade them. "Look at that sky—not a cloud in it," she said, gesturing upward. "You don't have anything to worry about. It's *definitely* not going to rain."

Millington High School was built in the style of a Spanish hacienda, its four wings enclosing a central courtyard. That courtyard was swarming with students now, all hurrying to deposit books in lockers before heading toward the gym. Willard Pugh threaded his way through the masses, greeting a few students but ignoring most, his attention focused on picking up every stray piece of toilet paper that blew across the grass or the concrete walkways. As he gathered the offending litter, he wadded it into a ball and shoved it into one of the large patch pockets that adorned the coat of his suit. Soon his pockets bulged like a squirrel's cheek full of nuts.

"Good morning, ladies," he said as he passed Martha and Beth. "Nice day for a pep rally." He didn't wait for a reply, but hurried on toward the gym.

" 'Good morning, ladies. N-a-s-s day for a pep rally.' " The voice did a wicked imitation of Willard Pugh's twang, then went on in a more natural tone. "Move it, Clara. You should be at your job station already."

Beth whirled around in time to feel a strong arm slip around her furry waist. Jed Stuart was grinning down at her. Instinctively, she circled his waist, too, her heart slamming against her rib cage as if she'd just finished a workout for the track team.

"Y'all did a great job on the house last night," Jed said as the threesome headed toward the back parking lot where the football team, mascots, and cheerleaders were assembling for the grand entrance. "It really looked great. Who did the mirror?" Jed looked straight at Beth when he said this, and she knew without checking her own mirror that her face was scarlet.

"Oh, Beth did that. Didn't you like it?" Martha was smiling now, as Beth's jaw dropped in astonishment. Before she could protest, Carl appeared and changed the subject. "I hear Woodrow went on a rampage last night," he said.

"They painted up the street in my neighborhood and messed up Larry's sign," Beth said. "I didn't know about anything else."

"Hah. They painted more than streets. There're eagle tracks on the back parking lot here, and they tore up a bunch of signs the Misses made. You didn't know about it?" he asked the group in general.

"My house survived," Jed said.

"Give me a break. Your dad's president of the school board. I can just see them painting up your place." Carl's voice was loaded with sarcasm. "The point is, we can't let them get away with this. We've got to get even."

"Don't look at me," said Jed. "I'll get benched if I do anything. You know that."

Carl shrugged. "Woodrow's going to feel our presence. You can count on that."

Jed looked at Beth. "I've gotta go, Clara old girl. Find me at lunch. There's something I want to ask you." He didn't wait for an answer, but gave Beth a playful pat on her furry backside and trotted off to join his teammates, who were gathering in a group behind the band.

Beth settled the papier-mâché cougar head over her own. Safe inside the mask, she allowed herself to stare at Jed as he left. She watched the way the muscles in his back moved underneath the cotton knit of his shirt as he ran toward the team. The place where Jed patted her still tingled, and slippery feelings—exciting and uncomfortable all at once—rolled around inside her like the balls of mercury from a broken thermometer. In order to get rid of them, Beth concentrated on the sounds coming from the Millington Marching Band.

The cadences from the band were deafening now, magnified in the crisp, clear air. Drums throbbed and cymbals clashed. The band broke into a rendition of "When the Saints Go Marching In," and the senior boys began to undulate across the parking lot, scuffing and scraping their feet across the alien eagle tracks and singing, "Oh, when those Coogs, go marching in; oh, when those Coogs go marching in . . ."

Toward the back of the parking lot, the last of the morning's buses rolled in and disgorged its cargo of noisy students. Beth could see some of Ruthanne's friends running toward the gym to get ready for the pep rally. Two of the boys from special education were fussing around the base of the flag pole. It was their job each day to raise and lower the American and Texas flags, and their faces wore looks of utter concentration as they carefully unfolded the triangular packages of cloth and attached them to the halyard. The flags slowly rose, then snapped and fluttered in the crisp morning breeze. The boys smiled at each other in satisfaction, and Beth felt a kind of electric shock of happiness. She looked around the campus of Millington and realized that this place was home to her, as dear and familiar as her own bedroom, populated with people who were like family, people whom she loved and felt connected to because they, too, loved Millington. She moved across the parking lot to take her place beside Carl, who bowed gallantly from his waist. Beth dropped a curtsy in return, and the football team roared its approval.

"Oh, when those Coogs, go marching in . . ." Everyone moved forward at the sound of the band director's whistle. Despite their heavy costumes, Beth and Carl began dancing, and occasionally somersaulting, at the head of the procession. The pep rally had begun.

CHAPTER

FOUR

In preparation for the traditional "run-through" of the football team, a paper screen painted with paw prints and slogans such as "Go Coogs," "Stomp Woodrow," and "We're #1" had been stretched across the open double doorway at the back of the Millington gym. Beth and Carl waited behind the screen now, anticipating the drumroll. The familiar excitement rippled through Beth, and she reached for her partner's furry paw. This was the moment she treasured the most—as far as she was concerned, the best part of being one of the mascots. The cymbals crashed; she and Carl took a running leap and burst through the screen.

Hundreds of students, jammed like sardines into the bleachers that lined the sides of the gym, exploded into frenzied screaming at the first tear of the paper and glimpse of the two mascots. They pounded their feet until the bleachers throbbed, and screamed, "Whip Woodrow; Whip Woodrow; Whip Woodrow." Buoyed by the spirit of the rally, Beth felt that she was floating as she and Carl separated and waltzed around opposite sides of the gym, urging the students on to more noise, more cheers, more chants.

The band marched in next. The brass section played the familiar melody but was almost drowned out by Millington voices singing, "Oh, when those Coogs, come marching in; oh, when those Coogs come marching in . . ." And then the Millington Cougars entered the gym like conquering heroes. Thunderous applause, catcalls, and foot stomping filled the air. Someone on the top row had a copper cowbell and began to ring it. Although the practice had been banned—at least in theory—showers of green and black confetti, like low-flying fireworks, appeared from everywhere, tossed down on the team by enthusiastic students—and some parents.

Beth and Carl somersaulted and danced with each other. Then Carl made an elaborate stage bow to Beth and worked his way out of the gym. It was time to roll in the Crouching Cougar, Millington's official mascot, a plaster statue that normally sat in the hall in front of Mr. Pugh's office. Once the cougar was in place, Beth knew pandemonium would reign again until everyone calmed down to sing the alma mater.

As she made her way along the perimeter of the gym, encouraging the noise to continue, Beth looked up into the stands and saw Adelaide Stuart sitting with Willard Pugh. Mrs. Stuart was dressed in a green sweater and she was waving a green-and-black pompom, just like the cheerleaders. As Beth danced by she waved enthusiastically, and Beth waved back. When Jed took his place with the team, Mrs. Stuart screamed "Get 'em, Jed" at the top of her lungs and shook her pom-pom furiously. Beth thought Jed looked embarrassed as he lifted his hand to acknowledge his mother's greeting. Jed Sr. pushed his way along the crowded bleacher and squeezed himself in beside his wife, just as the last member of the team took his seat in the reserved section of the bleachers. Beth watched as Jed's parents whispered greetings to each other. Mr. Stuart caught his son's eye and gave him a "thumbs up" victory sign; then he, too, joined in the waving and cheers.

Beth danced until her breathing was heavy and her heart was pounding more than usual. Something was wrong. The cheerleaders had made too many circles of the gym, and so had she. Inside the cougar head, beads of perspiration trickled down her temples.

Beth turned herself around to face the doorway. At any second she expected to see Carl pulling the cougar toward it, but no one was in sight. Tattered paper from the run-through clung to part of the door frame, giving it a forlorn look, like a broken piñata. The rest of the carefully painted sign had been ground into trash on the gym floor. Where was Carl? Just then, as if to answer her question, Beth saw him coming, and she danced in his direction. This was the cue the band's director had waited for; he raised his baton and the band began the sugary sweet melody of the alma mater, "Millington, Our Millington." Automatically, the student body rose to its feet and began to sing.

"What's going on?" Beth was panting and could barely manage to speak, but it didn't matter—Carl acted as if he hadn't heard her, anyway. The Crouching Cougar was nowhere in sight, and Carl stalked past Beth and across the gym floor, heading directly for Willard Pugh. Beth stared after him and watched while he scribbled something on a piece of borrowed notebook paper, then passed it up through the bleachers to Mr. Pugh. The principal looked surprised when the note reached him, but he quit singing and accepted it. He read it quickly, frowned, then handed the note to Mr. Stuart, who scanned it and shook his head in obvious disgust.

Beth stood at her post, singing automatically and mindlessly. Within a moment, Willard Pugh, accompanied by Jed Stuart, Sr., climbed out of the bleachers and came down on the gym floor to talk to Carl. Most of the students continued to sing about loyalty and friendship and honor within the hallowed halls of Millington, while Carl's arms flailed around as he talked to the two adults. A flash of light drew Beth's attention. One of the reporters from the local paper took a picture.

Beth saw Jed Sr. frown and shake his head in the direction of the reporter. The muscles in Willard Pugh's jaws hardened into visible bulges and Beth saw a red flush start in his neck and come up over his cheeks. ". . . dear Millington, for you." The last strains of the alma mater rose and faded, replaced by a deathly silence. All eyes were on the principal. The heels of his cowboy boots made loud clomping sounds on the polished hardwood of the gym floor as he strode briskly toward the portable microphone that was set up under the basketball hoop at the north end.

He took the microphone in his hand and held it gingerly. "I'm afraid . . . uhhh . . . I have some rather bad news." He cleared his throat loudly and slipped a finger inside the collar of his shirt, as if he needed to make more breathing room. "Carl here has informed me that the Crouching Cougar, symbol of Millington High School since it was founded fifteen years ago, is, uhhhh, missing from its customary spot in front of my office. I expect this is the work of some of our rivals who . . ."

"Woodrow! Woodrow! Woodrow!" The sound of the students chanting reminded Beth of prison riots she had seen in the movies. Willard Pugh held his hand up, and the gym fell silent once again.

"Now, we don't know that for certain. We don't know that at all. This school has rivals within our district and without."

Someone in the gym shouted, "We know who did it," and soon a chorus of "We know, we know, we know" filled the room until Mr. Pugh spoke directly into the microphone. "Y'all be quiet!" When the noise subsided, he went on.

"I think all of you know me well enough to understand that I don't hold with thievery. But I don't hold

41

with vengeance, either. I'm sure whoever did this will be caught and properly disciplined. Now, I know you're all hurt by this . . . so am I. But we don't have to take it lying down. No indeedy. Ours is a crouching cougar, and he's eternally ready to attack. I expect us to attack and get our revenge on the football field next Saturday night. We'll recover our cougar—and our pride—on that date like the champions we are. Am I right?"

A roar like an approaching tornado filled the gym, and in response, Martha and the other cheerleaders began a chant—"Get 'em back, get 'em back, harder, and harder. Get 'em back, get 'em back, harder, and harder." It was a parody of the chant—"push 'em back, push 'em back"—that was popular when the defense team took the field, and it didn't take long for the student body to catch on to the new words. Soon the gym reverberated with the sound. Beth caught a glimpse of Ruthanne up in the stands—so she'd come to the rally, after all. Even she was chanting, and Beth smiled broadly. School spirit was catching. She stole a quick glance at Mr. Pugh and Mr. Stuart. Both men were chanting along with everyone else, "Get 'em back, get 'em back, harder, and harder."

When everyone tired of the chant, the head coach took the microphone and introduced each of the players on the team. Then he introduced his four assistants and the trainer. After a few final cheers, the first bell rang. The pep rally was over, and the academic day had begun.

*   *   *

The missing cougar was the topic of conversation in most of the classrooms, and teachers brought students back to the subject at hand only by threats of detentions. Beth's government teacher passed out his quiz and called a halt to the classroom conversation. "The way you kids act, you'd think Woodrow kids were the Japanese and we were the navy at Pearl Harbor. It's time we got back to work."

By lunch, students were talking of nothing but the missing mascot. Beth, carrying her tray of spaghetti, threaded her way past the freshman tables, and Ruthanne, who rarely if ever even acknowledged her older sister's presence in the cafeteria, frantically waved. Beth walked over to her table. "You called?" she said with a half-smile.

"My friends and I want to know who took our cougar," Ruthanne said. Beth always knew when Ruthanne was showing off, and she was doing it now. It irritated Beth and she momentarily considered putting her sister down in front of her friends, then thought better of it. Instead, Beth took in the entire table of freshmen with a glance and said, "Your guess is as good as mine."

"The whole school's talking about it," Ruthanne said. "How'd they get it? That thing's heavy!"

"I'm sure it wasn't just one person," Beth answered.

"Well, we're going to get even, that's for sure," said a boy who was sitting at the end of the table.

"You'd better leave that to the seniors," Beth said as she moved toward the part of the cafeteria where the seniors ate. As she wound her way through the tables a couple of sophomores called out to Beth, "We'll get even, Clara. Just wait and see." Beth nodded and smiled at the boys, neither of whom she knew.

A familiar voice called from across the room. "Wait up, Beth. I told you I had something I wanted to talk to you about." Jed playfully punched one of his buddies on the arm in a kind of farewell gesture, then fell into step with Beth. "Boy, this is going to be some game and some weekend now, isn't it? I've never seen this school so riled up."

"Neither have I." Beth followed him to an empty table.

Jed deftly hooked a chair with his foot. "Have a seat," he said as he pulled another chair out for himself. "Want to be my date for the after-game dance? Well, for the game, too, for that matter." Jed's tone was as casual and confident as if he'd asked her to pass the salt. He slid a mixture of catsup and mayonnaise back and forth across his hamburger bun while he waited for her answer.

Beth rolled strands of spaghetti around her fork. The inside of her mouth felt as if it were lined with Kleenex, and she struggled to make her voice sound as casual as Jed's when she answered. "You mean this week's game—the one against Woodrow?" The minute she said it, she was sorry.

"That does seem to be the game that everyone's talking about," Jed said. "And I thought that's who we were playing."

Beth felt her cheeks redden.

"Of course I mean this week's game," he said, this

time in a kinder tone of voice. "I won't be much of a date for it, since I'll be playing, but a bunch of the guys on the team are going to get their dates to sit together. You could sit with them."

Beth was amazed. Apparently he had forgotten that she would be performing as Clara Cougar all night. Martha's words came back to her. "Jed's too stuck on Jed to do anything more than play the field." Was he too stuck on himself to notice what anyone else did for Millington? Beth swallowed a mouthful of food and said, "I'd like that, Jed, but I can't sit with everyone else. I'll be down on the field myself, remember?"

Jed winced and hit the heel of his hand against his head in an exaggerated gesture. "Sorry. I forgot. No problem, though. We'll just get together after the game and go on to the dance. How's that?" He didn't seem to expect an answer. He just took an enormous bite of his hamburger, and raised his fist in a salute to someone whom he had spotted across the cafeteria.

Beth managed to get out "Just fine" before Martha and a half-dozen other students dropped their trays and themselves at the table Jed and Beth were sharing.

Without any preamble, Martha looked at the assembled group and said to no one in particular, "Well, what are we going to do? We've got to get that cougar back before the game. The entire student body is looking to us to do it. Somebody said they heard that Woodrow's going to paint the cougar red and yellow and drag it out at halftime. I personally refuse to be humiliated like that in front of all those snotty kids at Woodrow. I just won't cheer if we don't have it back before the game. So there." Martha added emphasis to her last words with a nod of her head.

Martha's words stirred everyone at the table, and there were murmurs of "That's right" and "A-men!" A few more seniors crowded onto the bench to catch what Martha was saying, and Beth could feel Jed's arm press against hers in the crush.

She looked at Martha and said, "Calm down. How could anybody really know what they're going to do with the cougar? It's only been missing a few hours. Who told you?"

"Let's just say I have it on good authority," Martha said primly. "And anyway, just the fact that those creeps over there had the gall . . . the gall . . . to come in here and take something that belongs to us. It just . . . just enrages me. Carl's gone over to Woodrow now." Martha was sputtering as her indignation rose.

"Carl left the campus?" Beth was incredulous. Millington had strict rules about leaving the campus without permission. "How'd he get a pass?"

"Oh Beth, sometimes you amaze me. He didn't. He has a free period right before lunch, and he's supposed to work in the library, but Mrs. Shakley never notices anything. He just left."

"Well, that was stupid. If he's caught he'll be thrown in detention till next May." Beth took a bite of her spaghetti.

"He's not going to get caught. Friendly Fanny will let him back in. I've already talked to her."

Fanny Longoria was the parking lot guard. She was hired to protect the faculty's cars and to be certain that no student vehicles left the parking lot during school hours without a pass from the office. Upon occasion, Fanny was known to look the other way when a student left during lunch—especially if the culprit brought her a Big Mac on his return.

Jed swallowed the last of his hamburger and shook his head in admiration. "I tell you what, Martha. We ought to have you design some new plays for the team, or something. You think of everything, don't you? Dot every *i* and cross every *t*."

"I even reminded Carl to bring Fanny a McD.L.T. That's her latest kick." Martha looked around the table, expecting—and getting—approving nods from everyone. "I'm a stickler for detail. My dad says I'll be the perfect accountant."

"Or Mafia chief. Sorry, I'm just kidding." Jed ducked as Martha pretended to flip a spoon at him. Then he pushed his chair back and stacked his empty plates on the tray in front of him. He looked at Beth's plate. Her spaghetti had barely been touched. "Aren't you going to eat more than that?" he said.

"No. I'm not hungry," she replied. "I think I'm going to go outside and see if Carl's back yet. I don't want him to get into trouble—I need a partner for the game."

"I'll go with you," Martha said. "I want to be one of the first to find out what he knows."

"We'll all go," said Jed.

They carried their trays to the back of the cafeteria. Beth scraped the spaghetti into the plastic-lined garbage pail and slid her tray under the pass-through to

47

the kitchen. Dishes clattered and utensils clanked and the smell of steam, soap, and already-ripening garbage floated out the opening.

"Gad, it stinks in there," Martha said. "I don't know how they stand it."

"It's a job, and jobs are hard to come by these days," said Jed.

A vision of her father flashed into Beth's brain, but she pushed it back and hurried out of the cafeteria with the others. She was eager to get out into the cool clear air of the courtyard. Carl appeared almost immediately, strolling around the corner as casually as if he'd just returned from a trip to the boys' restroom.

"What'd you find out?" Martha asked the question for all of them.

"It's those scums from Woodrow—that's for sure," he said. "I'm gonna get it back before the game if it's the last thing I do. I'm going to get it back, or they're going to pay. I already left them a little down payment." Carl held his hand up. "Pssst," he said, and he sprayed an imaginary can of paint through the air.

"If I were you, man, I'd wash my hands. You've got green paint on your palm." Jed shifted the weight of his books from one hip to the other as he talked. Then he dropped his arm casually around Beth's shoulders and said, "I'll call you later," and headed off in the direction of his next class.

Martha watched Jed leave, then turned to Carl, who had spit on his palm and was rubbing the paint with his thumb. "You should have kept your mouth shut—at least in front of Jed. He doesn't need to know what you did." Martha put her arms around Carl's and Beth's shoulders and pulled them into a semi-huddle. "But just between us, what did you do?" she asked, laughing.

"I just took care of a few of their fancy eagles, that's all. Nobody saw me, don't worry. We'll liberate the cougar later. They're not going to get away with this." Carl's eyes were flashing—he thrived on this kind of excitement. "Everybody meet at my house tonight at eight. Spread the word. All seniors at my house at eight."

❧ *CHAPTER* ❧

F I V E

"You have any trouble getting out tonight?" Martha was twisting the dial on the radio impatiently as Beth slid into the station wagon. "Nobody plays any decent music anymore," she said.

"That's good. Leave it there," Beth said, pulling the visor down and checking her makeup in the mirror that was mounted behind it. "Everything was pretty smooth. Mom went to a committee meeting and Ruthanne's at the library. Dad just told me to be in by ten."

"Did you tell him what happened with the cougar?" Martha asked.

"Not exactly," Beth said slowly. "I told him that the seniors were going to have a planning session for the game this weekend, and I sort of mentioned that Woodrow had our mascot."

"What'd he say about it?" Martha asked.

"Nothing. He just told me when to be in and to be careful . . . the usual stuff."

"Don't worry. We'll be careful all right," Martha said as she pulled onto Carl's street. It was lined with cars, but Martha found a parking place near the end of the block and expertly maneuvered the long station wagon into it. "C'mon. We're late," she said as she slammed the car door shut. Both girls hurried down the street toward the Loessings' house.

"I wonder if Jed will be here?" Beth tried to sound nonchalant as they walked up the Loessings' driveway.

Martha looked at her closely and smiled knowingly. "Not a chance to see Romeo tonight, fair Juliet. The football players have been officially warned. No retaliation or they're kicked off the team. Coach Killough said so."

"I wonder if that goes for the mascots, too? Nobody said anything to me or Carl."

"Then I wouldn't worry about it," Martha said over her shoulder as she hurried through the gate that led into Carl's backyard. There were kids everywhere. Some were off in corners talking among themselves, but most were crowded around the Loessings' pool, shouldering themselves to its edge so they could better hear Carl, who stood on the diving board, finish his explanation of the evening's plan. Martha and Beth stood at the edge of the crowd, but Carl saw them immediately.

"Hey, Beth!" He waved a green pepper in greeting, then continued to toss it from hand to hand as he completed his instructions. "Now, does everybody have it? Me, Todd, Andy, and Brian are going after the cougar. The rest of you are on your own. Todd, you have the rest of the peppers?"

A voice from the back of the crowd answered. "Three cases. I went to four different Safeways to get them. I told one manager I was in charge of a church supper—told him we were going to have stuffed peppers."

The crowd laughed appreciatively. "We're going to stuff some peppers all right," Carl said. Beth felt a twinge of apprehension at the tone in his voice. She glanced over the crowd, then turned to Martha and said, "I haven't seen half of these people before. Who are they?"

"Oh, they're Millington kids. They just don't do much around the school, but I've seen them—most of them are a bunch of potheads."

The crowd was dispersing now, everyone heading toward the cars in the street. Beth and Martha watched the boy called Todd get two other kids to help him load the green peppers into the back of a pickup truck. As the crowd thinned Beth saw several of the girls from the Misses. They smiled and waved at her. Seeing them made Beth feel much better and she smiled and waved back. Martha called to Susan Pendergast and Marie Arcola, who were getting into a car together. "See you at Woodrow." She gave two cheerful toots on the car's horn.

Martha made one detour on her way to the school. Beth waited in the car until her friend emerged from Grotard's Hardware carrying several cans of green and black spray paint which she tossed in the front seat between herself and Beth.

"What are you going to do with those?" Beth asked—a pointless question, since she knew the answer in advance.

"Paint Fido's dog house. What do you think I'm going to do with them?"

"Nothing, I hope. Martha, I thought we were just going to get our own property back, not paint up Woodrow. That makes us just as bad as they are. And besides, we could get into real trouble."

"This is war. 'No quarter given' and 'tit for tat' is all I have to say." Martha looked at Beth, who was staring straight ahead and frowning.

"We're gonna get killed, is what I say," Beth answered.

Martha drove the car slowly around the long oval drive that led to Woodrow Wilson High School. The car's headlights shone on freshly painted yellow eagle tracks that marched across the drive's asphalt surface in an orderly pattern, then ran up the two utility poles that stood at either end of the oval. "Look how neat they are," Beth said, craning to get a better look at them.

"Can you imagine Pee-U ever letting us do that kind of stenciling on the city light poles? We can only put our paws on the Parents' Drive." Martha's nostrils flared delicately, and her mouth turned down at the corners as she mentioned Mr. Pugh's name.

Beth gazed aimlessly over the part of Woodrow's campus she could see from the drive. Like Millington, it sat on acreage that was studded with pine and oak trees. And like Millington, those trees were draped in toilet paper. Paper banners painted in red and yellow hung from the school's mustard-colored brick walls, proclaiming the supremacy of the Woodrow Eagles. Woodrow looked like any other high school in Fort Preston right before a big football game, and yet something didn't feel right. Quiet, dark, bathed in moonlight—Woodrow had an eerie, almost alien, appearance. Beth turned to Martha and said, more curtly than she intended, "Nobody's here. Let's just go home."

Martha gave her a sharp look. "Don't be ridiculous!" she said. "Nobody's here because they're all parked over at Pine Ridge Center. You don't think anybody's going to be dumb enough to park on this campus, do you? We're going there."

Pine Ridge Shopping Center lay just to the north of Woodrow Wilson High School, separated from the school's property only by a hedge of Ligustrum bushes. It was two minutes away by car, or a forty-five-second walk if you chose to slip through the hedge. The gaps in the hedge attested to the traffic between the high school and the shops that made up the center.

Martha pulled into the Pine Ridge parking lot and carefully slotted the giant car between two others parked in front of the Piggly-Wiggly store. In the store's main window, a life-sized cardboard cheer-leader, complete with megaphone and pom-poms, stood ready to leap into the air. A sign announced that Piggly-Wiggly was football headquarters, "Your stop for mums and after-game party supplies." To reinforce this message, cartons of Dr. Pepper, Coke, and 7-Up were stacked beside bins containing pretzels, chips, nuts, and candy. The bins were decorated with red and yellow corrugated cardboard borders with wavy edges—the kind teachers use to trim classroom bulletin boards. Red and yellow swags and loops of crepe paper hung in the windows, and instead of the usual "Special . . . Chickens, 39 cents a pound" someone had painted "Go Eagles!! Good luck from all your friends at Piggly-Wiggly!!"

Todd's pickup truck was parked in front of the toy store. Beth noticed that its passengers and the crates of peppers were already gone. Other cars pulled into the center. Millington students poured out of them. Some called greetings to Martha and Beth, and others ig-nored them, hurrying on toward Woodrow's campus. Everyone behaved as naturally as possible, not want-ing to attract any unnecessary attention. Beth behaved as casually as the rest, returning waves and greetings as if they were all running into each other quite by accident.

The center was dominated by a branch office of Franklin O'Connor's bank. A large clock, mounted in a cupola above the bank, bonged once, and Beth looked up. It was 8:30. In the distance, a whistle sounded, and within a moment, a freight train roared along the tracks that ran just north of the center. It thundered off into the night, and Beth felt inexplicably lonely as the sound faded into the distance.

"Let's go. Everybody's already over at Woodrow." Martha's voice was urgent. She stuffed two cans of paint into her purse.

"I'm ready," Beth answered, deliberately shaking off the lonely feeling. They pushed through the hedge, and Martha headed toward the Woodrow field house with Beth following. Both girls walked hurriedly, but silently, in the cold, clear night.

Every high school in the district had a field house where athletic equipment was stored and the coaches had their offices. Woodrow's sat on the edge of the football practice field, separated from the main campus by Dover Lane, a quiet residential street. "Look!" Martha said, pointing to eagle tracks on Dover Lane that had been all but obliterated with green paint. "I bet that's what Carl did today," she said with satisfaction.

The two girls were across Dover now, heading toward the field house, when suddenly its door flew open and two senior boys rushed past them.

"I thought sure it'd be in there," Beth heard one say to the other, a tall red-headed kid who had warmed the bench during last week's football game. Beth didn't get a good look at the other boy before both were gone, heading at a dead run toward Woodrow's main campus.

Susan Pendergast and Marie Arcola followed the

two boys out of the field house. Both girls carried cans of spray paint, and Marie said, "Wait a minute, I'm gonna get this wall."

"Marie, don't!" The words came out of Beth's mouth as if they had a life of their own, and she was as surprised at uttering them as Marie was at hearing them.

"Well, well, listen to you," Marie said, then pointed the can of green spray paint at the wall of the field house and spewed out "Woodrow sucks" in a large snakelike script. Beth heard a ripping sound, then laughter—low and gutteral—coming from inside the building. Quietly, she and Martha walked to the doorway and looked inside. Two figures—boys—were slicing the covers of the gym mats. Beth's heart was beating wildly and her feet itched to run, run, run. She reached a hand out to Martha and tugged on her arm. "This is trouble," she said. "Who are they, do you know?"

Martha looked shaken, but she quickly recovered her composure. "I don't know, but they don't have anything to do with us. Let's catch up with Marie and Susan." She took off and Beth—glad to run somewhere, anywhere—quickly followed.

Martha, Marie, and Susan made it across Dover Lane before a flurry of cars stopped Beth. When the cars had passed and Beth was free to cross, the others had disappeared from sight. Beth darted across the street and ran quickly along the drive in front of the school. The air smelled pungent and spicy. Green peppers by the dozens were crushed all over the yellow eagle claws on the oval drive. Someone had thrown green peppers at the front doors of Woodrow. They lay bruised and cracked on the steps, and a few white seeds still clung to the glass insets in the doors. Close by, she could hear laughter and a soft kind of popping sound as the overripe vegetables exploded against the walls and driveways of the school. A crash, then the sound of tinkling glass. A girlish voice, familiar to Beth, said, "Oops, my aim never was very good!" A disembodied voice, this time male, said, "They didn't stash it there, either, but at least in the morning they'll know we came to call." Laughter rippled through the night air and footsteps thudded off through the pines.

Beth rounded the corner, searching for Martha, or Marie and Susan, in every knot of kids she saw. In the distance lay the tennis courts and she jogged in that direction. Two boys she didn't recognize were standing by the net on Court A, arguing.

"I say slash the whole net," said one.

"Naah," said the other. "Let's just cut it down," and to Beth's horror, they produced a wicked-looking knife with a curved blade and did exactly that. She ran, on and on, dodging pine trees, not stopping to acknowledge the greetings of those she knew. The lonely feeling that had started in the parking lot grew stronger, then changed into real fear.

Where was Martha? As she approached the vocational education building she saw Marie and Susan spraying a car with green *M*'s for Millington. Martha was on the other side of it, painting something on the door. She tossed a can of green paint to Beth, whose hand instinctively opened for the catch. "Here, get the trunk," she said.

"What am I supposed to do with the trunk?" Beth asked. "We need to get out of here."

"Paint something on it," Susan said. "My brother's best friend goes here. He told me they use this old heap for their unit on body-painting. We're just helping them along, that's all."

"That's right, we're just doing them a service," said Martha. "Go ahead, Beth, give the trunk a stripe of green or something. It doesn't hurt anything. They're just going to paint over it next semester, anyway."

Marie and Susan were working on one of the fenders, which, Beth noticed, already had a hodge-podge of colors on it, as if someone were testing swatches.

"I don't know," Beth said, hesitating.

"What's the matter, O'Connor? No guts? Put something immortal right there on the trunk, and make it quick. You're right about one thing—it's getting late, and we need to go."

The can of spray paint felt hot in Beth's hand, and she held it as if it were a hand grenade with the pin pulled out. She walked around the car, perched on its concrete blocks, buying time and waiting for inspiration. A carefully stenciled Woodrow eagle spread its wings across the hood, and for a moment Beth considered doing something to it, but somehow she didn't want to.

Marie and Susan had finished with the sides of the

car. "It's your turn," Susan said, throwing a challenging look at Beth.

"Give me a minute, I'm thinking," Beth said irritably. Suddenly, it came to her. "How about, 'Within this trunk, rotting in the sun, lies the carcass of an Eagle, Millington's Number One!' "

"That's just wonderful," Marie squealed. "I don't know how you ever thought of it."

Beth didn't know how she thought of it, either, but she was pleased with herself. "If I just had some feathers, I'd glue them to the edge of the trunk . . . just for effect." In the excitement of the moment, the sagging tennis nets and sound of broken glass had slipped from her mind.

"Too bad it won't even *be* here next week," said Susan. "The maintenance people always clean this stuff up the next day. They sandblast the walls and everything. I remember when my brother's class did a bunch of stuff to Valleybrook a few years ago. He tried to take me over there the next day and show me, but it was already gone."

"See, Beth?" said Martha triumphantly. "It's nothing permanent, anyway. Here today, gone tomorrow . . . like writing in the sand."

The creamy expanse of trunk lid stretched out in front of her. Beth pressed the nozzle of the spray can and a stream of green paint sputtered out and ran down her hand and arm. She wiped the paint off on her jeans and tried again. This time, it came out properly and she began to write across the trunk. She got as far as "rotting" when several boys raced by. "Cops!" they shouted. "Get out of here!"

Suddenly dozens of kids were running across the open field behind the vocational ed building. They ran like scattering mice, some vaulting over chain link fences into the darkened back yards of the homes that bordered the Woodrow property on the eastern side. Some ran toward the spot where Beth stood transfixed. "You'd better get going," Todd and Andy shouted as they sped past.

"Every woman for herself," Martha said over her shoulder as she began to race toward the homes that lay ahead. "I'll meet you at the car."

Beth was disoriented, in an unfamiliar part of the Woodrow campus, and panic pushed her. She considered following Martha for a brief instant, but instinct told her the shopping center and the safety of the car lay in the opposite direction. She ran as if a pack of frenzied dogs were chasing her and snapping at her heels.

Finally she came again to the familiar oval drive. Her side ached and she stopped, gasping for breath. The night was silent and cold. No one—no cops or kids—was in sight. For a moment Beth wondered if this was somebody's idea of a joke. Maybe there hadn't been any cops. She hadn't seen any . . . just kids running. Beth looked down at her feet. Her white sneakers were stained with grass and the pulp from dozens of pureed green peppers. She stooped to scrape some of the mess off the soles of her shoes, then she heard thudding footsteps behind her.

Beth whirled around and saw Carl and John Bartlett. John was Jed's best friend, and Millington's best receiver, the one Jed counted on to complete his passes. She opened her mouth to ask John what he, a football player, was doing here, but Carl shook his head furiously and held a finger over his lips to silence her. Without a word the three of them began to run toward Pine Ridge Center. As Beth ran she breathed a silent prayer, "Please, God, let Martha be there."

"Stop right there. Police." The voice on the bull horn stopped the three students in mid-step, while a spotlight pinned them in place. Irrationally, Beth thought of the stories she had heard her grandfather tell about alligator hunting in the bayous of Louisiana when he was a child; how he and his daddy before him had taken a lantern and a shotgun and gone out, late at night, to hunt the creatures. "That light'd freeze them suckers dead in their tracks. All you had to do is pick 'em off," he would say. Beth had always hated that story.

The spotlight snapped off, but the red and white lights on top of the patrol car continued to whirl around in an odd kind of light show. As the two officers approached, Beth noticed that their hands rested lightly on top of their gun butts. One policeman, the younger of the two, pulled his hand away from the gun when his eyes met Beth's.

"You kids been trashing up this school?" the older one said to no one in particular.

"No sir," said Carl with conviction. "We just came over here to see what was going on."

"You go to school here? You here to protect your own property?" The policeman turned his head and expertly expelled a stream of brownish spittle that landed with a sickening splat on the driveway. Beth felt the bile rise in her throat; she closed her eyes and forced herself to swallow.

The three of them remained silent.

"I'll ask the young lady. Where do you go to school, ma'am?" The policeman's tone of voice was too patient—exaggeratedly so. He smirked, and Beth concentrated on the bulge in his left cheek. "Millington," she answered. Her voice sounded foreign to her own ears, as if she were speaking under water.

"Oh-h-h, ho! Millington kids! The old rivalry at work, is that it? I went to Valleybrook myself." It was the younger officer talking now. Beth noticed the hint of a smile around his face, and she felt strangely comforted that he had attended a high school in the area. Surely he would understand about football, and mascots, and school spirit.

Carl was speaking now. "Uh, Woodrow . . . uh, Woodrow came over to our school over the weekend. They stole our cougar—right out of the building. They brought it over here somewhere. We just came to get it back . . . that's all, officer, I swear. We just came over here to get the cougar back."

The car radio crackled and the younger officer went to take the message. When he returned, the smile had left the corner of his mouth. "That was Car Seventy-two on the other side of the campus. Seems the tennis nets have been torn up, and a bunch of the equipment in the field house—tumbling mats, basketballs, footballs—is flat destroyed. School's painted up pretty bad, too. I told Hankins we had some kids in custody over here."

Beth stared hard at the young officer, trying to

anticipate what he was going to say next. He avoided looking directly at her. "Hankins used the car radio to patch into the school district's emergency number. Whoever took the call said to take the kids in. They're gonna press charges."

CHAPTER

S I X

Beth sat in the back of the police car, staring at the metal grill that separated Carl, John, and herself from the two officers in the front seat. The U-Tote-Em grocery, the library, the Exxon station at the corner— all the familiar landmarks of the area—passed by. Everywhere she looked, toilet paper hung from trees and paper banners clung to the brick walls that enclosed the different subdivisions. Even the streets in this part of Fort Preston were stenciled with yellow eagle claws. Absentmindedly, she picked at a stubborn streak of green paint that ran across the back of her hand; it refused to come off.

Eventually the familiar sights faded, and the neighborhoods became progressively seedier as the car headed downtown. The staccato and static-laced sounds of the police radio filled the car. "Suspected armed robbery in progress. Elam and Main." "Car Seventy-two proceed to Clearview Apartments. Two-nine-oh-one Gunter. Hostage being held at gunpoint." The violence of this night in Fort Preston was reported in bored, businesslike tones.

Beth was wedged between Carl, who was staring at his feet, and John, who looked out the window and constantly drummed his fingers on his thigh. The two officers in the front chatted casually about the fate of the Dallas Cowboys. Beth tried to swallow, but her throat was dry. Finally, she managed to whisper to Carl, "What do you think is going to happen?"

He lifted his head to look at Beth and shrugged his shoulders but said nothing. The self-confidence he had had earlier in the evening was gone, and Beth realized with a sinking feeling that Carl was as frightened as she.

At the station she was separated from the two boys and was searched, fingerprinted, photographed, and booked by herself. Eventually, a matron carrying a large manila envelope came into the room where she was being held. She looked Beth over and said, "Do you have a belt?"

When Beth shook her head, the matron opened the manila envelope and said, "Empty your pockets on the table over there. Put your watch over there, too. And your rings."

Beth did as she was told and watched as the matron carefully wrote the contents on the outside of the envelope, then put the gum, change, the watch her father had given her for her sixteenth birthday, and her senior ring into the envelope.

"What's going to happen to me?" Beth asked.

"That depends on what you've done, doesn't it?" the matron answered.

"Do you know what time it is? My parents will be worried sick. I need to call them."

The woman looked at her watch and said, "It's twelve-thirty."

"I was supposed to be home hours ago!" Beth almost cried. "I've got to make a phone call."

"You'll get to call in due time. Somebody'll come get you. I just check 'em in. You've got to come with me, at least for now."

The matron led Beth down a long corridor and through doors that opened at a punched-in code. A fetid smell of unwashed bodies and stale cigarette smoke assaulted Beth's nostrils as soon as she and the matron stepped inside. Her mouth began to salivate like it always did right before she threw up, and she swallowed vigorously, willing herself not to retch. Rows of tiny cells, almost all of them occupied, lined both sides of the corridor. Beth was escorted to one that wasn't much bigger than her mother's closet. The door clanged shut, and the matron walked away.

Jailed prisoners always paced. At least, that's what Beth had read, and she paced aimlessly now: four steps to the north, six to the west, trodding out the dimensions of her own tiny space. Finally, because she was exhausted, she overcame her revulsion and sat on the narrow cot that was pushed against one wall of her cell. The mattress was stained and the paint had chipped off sections of the cot's metal frame, leaving rusty metal spots. She sat on the very edge and hugged her arms to her, taking comfort from their familiar, solid feel. And she thought about home. Her mother had probably returned from her committee meeting by ten, wanting to know where Beth was. Her father had most likely looked up from his book and said, "Don't worry until you have something to worry about, Jo. She'll be home any minute." And if Ruthanne were anywhere nearby to witness this exchange, she'd complain that Beth always got to do things that she couldn't do. Well, Ruthanne certainly wouldn't want to be doing this.

Beth shifted her weight and absentmindedly lifted her wrist to look at her watch. Her tanned arm showed a white strip of skin where her watch had been. Tears of frustration welled again. Surely her parents were calling the police. Surely she would be out of here soon.

In the distance a door opened again and voices drifted back into the cell area. "You need to learn to control your students, Willard," a male voice said angrily.

"Now, Earl, I understand the gravity of all of this. I surely do. But I imagine central maintenance will get it cleaned up quick. Why, last year they had us sandblasted and cleaned up in jig time. These kids do get fired up during football, don't they?" Beth recognized Willard Pugh's twang. His voice was soothing, as if he were talking to a child. "Earl" would be Earl Harper, principal of Woodrow.

"Fired up enough that administration gets us up in the middle of the night to press charges . . ." The voices faded away.

Hope flooded through Beth. If the district was going to press charges, surely the principals would come and talk to her, and John, and Carl first. They'd want to have the full story—not just the police version. Then they'd realize that she was no delinquent and her parents would be called to take her home. Beth quickly ran her fingers through her hair—the only method she had of combing it—and stood in readiness.

The minutes ticked by. No one came for her. Weariness, like the force of gravity, pulled her down, and she lay on the cot and let her thoughts drift to Martha. Had she been arrested, too? Beth finally fell asleep, and the sun was shining outside the small, barred window when she awoke. Within a few minutes, a police officer was unlocking the cell door. "Your father is here for you," she said without any ceremony at all. Beth bolted from her cot and silently followed the woman back to the room where she had been booked.

Franklin O'Connor was signing some papers at the desk when Beth was escorted in. He looked up at her quickly, then pushed the papers across the desk to the sergeant. "Are you all right, Bethy?" he said, using her childhood nickname as he peered into her face.

Tears sprang into Beth's eyes and she nodded, not trusting herself to speak.

The matron tossed the envelope containing Beth's belongings onto a table. "Look them over, then sign this," she said, pushing a receipt and a ballpoint pen that said "AAA Bail Bonds. Dial F-R-E-E-D-O-M" at Beth.

She quickly scrawled her name on the receipt and strapped on her watch. It was eight-thirty A.M. Within five minutes, Beth and her father were walking together into the brilliant sunshine of this October morning, heading home.

"I'm sorry, Daddy," Beth said as soon as the two of them were in the privacy of the car and she trusted herself to speak. She noticed that her father had stubble all over his chin and he was still wearing the suit, minus the coat and tie, that he had had on last night.

Franklin O'Connor drew in his breath and blew it out forcefully. "It's a little late for 'sorry,' Beth. I thought you were going to some kind of a meeting. When you didn't come home and didn't call by ten-thirty, your mother began to worry and started imagining all kinds of things, but not this mess, I can assure you. You'd better tell me what happened and it had better make sense."

"I'm not sure, myself. We just went over to get the cougar back—Martha and I."

"When we called at eleven-thirty she was home in bed," Mr. O'Connor interrupted. "Her parents had no idea where you were. Are you telling me now that you and she were together? How come she wasn't arrested?"

Beth's mind whirled frantically. Had Martha denied being at Woodrow? "A lot of kids were over at Woodrow, Daddy. It wasn't just me who got arrested. Carl did, too. And so did John Bartlett. What's happened to them, do you know?"

"Carl's out. I don't know anything about the Bartlett boy. Carl's father is the one who let us know the police had you. He called around one-thirty, I guess. Your mother and I had already called the hospitals and the accident division of the police, looking for you." Mr. O'Connor shook his head. "As I said, it never occurred to us to check with the criminal division to see if you'd been arrested."

Franklin O'Connor looked at Beth with red-rimmed eyes. "We hated hearing this news from someone else. Why didn't you call us yourself, Beth?"

"They didn't let me, Daddy. I asked."

"That's crazy! Obviously Carl made his one phone call."

"It's not like you see on television. The matron said I'd have to wait till later. I figured someone would come to get me and let me call, but no one did. Mr. Pugh was there. So was Mr. Harper."

"They were? What time was that?" Franklin O'Connor said.

"I didn't have my watch, but it must have been around one o'clock. They didn't talk to me, either. Finally, I fell asleep." Irrationally, Beth felt angry. "Wait a minute. If you knew where I was at one-thirty, how come it took so long to get me out?"

"Give me a break, Beth," he said sharply. "It's taken

me all night to arrange your bail. I didn't want to use a bondsman—that would just cost more money—so I had to borrow some cash. I usually don't carry eight hundred around in pocket change, you know."

"I'm sorry," Beth whispered again.

Franklin O'Connor just shook his head. "Beth, I want the truth," he said. "What did you do to the school? I'm going to have to make it right, and I need to know." His voice was gravelly with lack of sleep and Beth noticed that her father's hands were gripping the steering wheel so tightly that his knuckles had turned white.

"I didn't do anything to the school, Dad, I promise. All I did was paint a few words on the trunk of a car."

"No!" The protest exploded from her father's mouth. "Whose car?"

"It doesn't belong to anybody," Beth said quickly. "It's a junk car they use for body-painting in vocational ed. It gets painted all the time. It didn't hurt anything, really."

"It didn't help," her father said. "The police say there's been wholesale destruction at Woodrow. Equipment destroyed and obscenities sprayed all over the walls of the field house. In green paint." He looked at Beth's arm, which still bore the telltale signs of green.

"Daddy, you're not blaming me for the walls, are you?" she exclaimed. "I wouldn't do that. You know I wouldn't."

"All I know is what I've been told," he said grimly. "And I've been told that there's been thousands of dollars worth of damage. Damage that you and Carl and John have been charged with."

"There couldn't have been that kind of damage done, I'm sure of it," Beth cried. Then she thought of the sagging tennis nets and the sounds of breaking glass, and she shuddered. "Does Ruthanne know?"

"Of course," her father replied. "She wanted to stay home from school, but your mother and I insisted that she go. She was pretty upset."

Beth's head was throbbing, and she leaned it against the window of the car. The cool glass felt good against her forehead, and she rode in silence the rest of the way home.

When they pulled into their driveway, Beth dropped her face into her cupped hands and rubbed her eyes. They were sore when she rubbed them, and her skin felt gritty. What she wanted most at this moment was sleep. A line from Shakespeare—one that she had been forced to memorize for English class—swam up from her subconscious: "Sleep, that knits up the raveled sleeve of care." That said it all. If she could just stay home from school and sleep she might be able to knit herself back together. Then perhaps she could make some sense of the events of last night.

Franklin O'Connor turned the key in the lock and the back door swung open. Barney danced around the two of them in spasms of glee.

"We've got her home, Jo," Franklin O'Connor called toward the back of the house, and Beth heard the hair dryer snap off. Joanne O'Connor, fresh from a shower and wrapped in a terry cloth robe, walked into the den. She finished twisting her still-damp hair into a knot on the back of her head, then sank into a corner of the sofa while she contemplated her daughter.

"Bethany Lynn, you will never know what you've put both of us through," she began. Beth stood there for a moment, then she murmured, "I know, Mother. I'm sorry."

"You were *arrested*. My daughter, the vandal. I just can't believe it. What can you possibly say for yourself?" Joanne O'Connor's eyes were brimming with angry, exhausted tears. Beth knew better than to try to offer an excuse, or even much of a detailed explanation. Punishment was coming, swift and sure. I'll probably be grounded till I'm forty, she thought to herself, then drew in her breath to answer.

"We just wanted to get our cougar back, that's all. Woodrow kids broke into Millington and stole it. I just went there to help get the cougar back. I didn't hurt anything."

"Did you have to do some painting to get it back?" Joanne asked, gesturing to the streak of green paint on Beth's hand.

"Sounds like she painted up an old car that was outside the vocational ed building," Franklin said.

"I didn't 'paint it up,' Dad. I just sprayed a few words."

" 'Flagrant vandalism' is the term the police used . . . or maybe it was the school district. They're the ones pressing charges," Franklin O'Connor said dully.

"We'll have to hire a lawyer, and go to court." Joanne's voice was cracking. "And we'll have to pay to have that car repainted . . . Lord knows what that will cost. This is a terrible mess." Joanne O'Connor dropped her head into her hands and began to massage her temples.

Mr. O'Connor broke the silence that hung in the room. "We'll talk finances later. It's been a rough night for all of us, and I, for one, am going to hit the showers. Beth, I'd suggest you do the same and get ready for school. I'll drop you off on the way to the bank." Franklin O'Connor walked out of the room, and Beth looked at her mother incredulously.

"School? I can't go to school after everything that happened last night. I've got an awful headache, and my eyes feel like they're lined with sandpaper. Don't make me go to school today. Please."

"Sorry, my dear. Ruthanne went, and you certainly will go and face everyone." Joanne O'Connor's tone was crisp and efficient now. "You should have thought about all of this before the impulse to become another Rembrandt hit."

"I know," Beth said miserably.

Abruptly, Beth's mother patted the sofa next to her. "Come sit down, Beth. We need to have a talk."

Beth collapsed into the opposite corner of the sofa and faced her mother.

"I know all the damage they're describing at Woodrow couldn't have been done by the three of you who were arrested," said Mrs. O'Connor. "It's physically impossible. Others were over there, and they should be held responsible for it, too. Martha had to be there. You and she left together."

75

"Forget who else was there, Mother," Beth said in a dull voice. "I don't rat on people."

Beth didn't want to continue the conversation along these lines, so she said, "I'm so tired I can hardly think, but I'll go grab a shower and be ready for school in fifteen minutes. Ask Dad to wait for me. Can we talk when I get home? I'll try to explain some things then."

"While you're explaining, explain how you're going to pay to get that car repainted," Mrs. O'Connor said, and she stood up and walked out of the room.

Beth scrubbed in the shower as if she wanted to wash away all that had happened. She began with the smears of paint on her arm and hand, scrubbing until the skin was red. She wondered how much it would cost to repaint that car. When Carl had gotten his Camaro repainted a few weeks ago, he said it cost five hundred dollars. Five hundred dollars was a lot of money to pay back. Well, she would just have to get a part-time job—maybe at Fanner's Department Store. Yes, that's what she'd do, she'd go to work at Fanner's. And Susan and Marie and Martha would have to kick in money, too. They'd simply have to. She'd tell them so this morning.

As soon as she decided to apply for work at Fanner's, Beth felt better. Reaching decisions always made her feel better—she was like her mother that way. She'd work it out. The shower water continued to pour over her, lifting her spirits as the green-tinged grime of the previous evening washed down the drain.

"Hustle along, Beth. I've got to get to work." Franklin O'Connor rapped on Beth's bedroom door as he walked briskly down the hall. Beth gave herself a final check in the mirror. She didn't look too bad. A bit of foundation hid any shadows that lingered under her eyes, and blush gave her cheeks some color. She gathered up her books and walked into the kitchen, where her parents were engaged in conversation.

". . . figure out something about the money later," her father was saying. He stopped short when Beth came into the room.

"I'm going to get a job, Dad. At Fanner's. I'll pay you back for what all this costs. It'll take time, but I'll do it."

Franklin O'Connor looked at Beth and smiled slightly. "It'll take quite a while with the salary at Fanner's, believe me. But I'll accept your offer, Beth. This hasn't come at a particularly good time for us. And I think some form of punishment is still in order, but I'm not sure what it should be. Standing trial at seventeen is punishment, but your mother and I will discuss other options, too."

Trial. Beth hadn't realized that she'd have to stand trial. Heretofore the thought of court had conjured up images of traffic violations and quick statements in front of a judge. But trials meant testimony and witnesses and juries. Now she really had to get to school. She needed to talk to Carl and John. Then there was Martha, and Susan, and Marie—she would talk to them, too, and maybe even Mr. Pugh. That was it. She'd talk to Mr. Pugh and explain how all this got started.

The phone in the kitchen rang, and Beth jumped at the sound. Franklin O'Connor picked up the receiver, and Beth tried to read his face as he spoke. "Yes. Well, I suppose so. One-thirty this afternoon. All right then. Good-bye."

He replaced the phone in its cradle gingerly, as if he were laying a bomb to rest. Joanne O'Connor and Beth stood waiting for him to speak, but he walked slowly into the den and sank into his favorite chair. Then, leaning his head back and closing his eyes, he said. "You might as well get some sleep, Beth. At least for a while. Your mother and you and I have an appointment with Willard Pugh at one-thirty. You've been suspended from school."

Joanne O'Connor sat tensely in the front seat of the car. "I need to have this straight in my mind before we face Mr. Pugh," she said. "Franklin, you saw the charges. Exactly what was Beth arrested for?"

Mr. O'Connor passed his hand across his forehead. "I've told you, Jo, at least fifty times. Criminal mischief."

"But Beth said she was just running across the campus when she was arrested. She wasn't doing anything at the time. Isn't that right, Beth?" She twisted herself around, looking to Beth for confirmation.

"Yeah, that's right, Mother. I wasn't doing anything when I was arrested, but remember, I did spray paint on the car."

"But the police don't know that, do they? I mean, that's not what you were arrested for? I'm just trying to get the picture of what happened clear in my mind. I'm sorry if I'm a slow study . . . I don't do well without sleep."

"Neither do I," said Beth. Her mother's mouth opened to say something, but before she could talk Beth hurried on. "I don't know whether the police know about the car or not. They didn't say anything about it—it happened a while before . . . before we were caught."

"Who else knows you painted on the car?" her mother said.

"I told you, Mother, I'm not going to tell on anybody. Just let me take my punishment and get it over with." Tears of frustration, anger, fear, and exhaustion burned Beth's eyes and threatened to trickle down her cheeks. She hadn't cried this much since she was five and broke her arm falling out of her grandfather's pecan tree.

Joanne O'Connor dug inside her purse and extracted a starched lacy handkerchief and offered it to Beth. Her mother was the only woman Beth knew who still carried handkerchiefs that had to be laundered. Beth dabbed the tears away. The handkerchief smelled of her mother's perfume; the smell and the scratchy feel of the fabric comforted Beth in a strange way. She folded the handkerchief and slipped it into her own purse, while her mother continued talking. "I just think the others should own up to being there, that's all. And I see no need for you to mention painting the car, unless you're asked directly about it, of course. Then you'll have to tell the truth. Remember, in this country you're innocent until proven guilty, and you don't have to testify against yourself. Didn't they tell you all that when they arrested you?"

"They didn't say anything when they arrested me," Beth said. Although she was exhausted, she still had the energy to be surprised at her mother's advice. She had assumed Mother expected her to confess fully as soon as she saw Mr. Pugh.

"They didn't read you your rights?" Joanne O'Connor was aghast.

"I guess they forgot," Beth answered. She turned her face to stare out the window. They were rounding the corner of Mulberry Street now, and within a minute the car pulled up in front of Millington. Beth was struck with the sheer normalcy of the scene in front of her. She couldn't have said what she expected—perhaps a pile of bricks and mortar where the Millington building had been. At the least, anxious knots of students and teachers discussing the events of last night, noticing that Beth was not among them this morning. Instead, the toilet paper swung gaily from the trees and the flags fluttered at the top of their poles. Although it was early afternoon, a few students waited, books in hand, by the Parents' Drive. Obviously they were getting picked up to go to doctor or dentist appointments. With some surprise, Beth realized that student life at Millington marched on without her.

As she got out of the car, Beth looked across the

campus to Millington's practice field. It was filled with a sea of green jerseys, and Beth strained to pick out number 59. While she stared, Jed and another boy—she couldn't make out who it was from this distance—emerged from the gym and trotted toward the field. They were laughing together; then they stopped for a moment and began to box playfully with each other. Their jerky, happy movements reminded Beth of puppets dancing on a string, and she smiled slightly. She felt better for having seen Jed.

The bell ending fifth period rang, and within minutes the campus was swarming with students heading to lockers and then to classes. Beth felt her father's hand cup her elbow. "Are you ready?" he said, propelling her toward the building's main entrance.

For the first time in all Beth's years there, Millington did not look welcoming, and she dreaded walking down those crowded halls. She wasn't as ready to face her friends as she had thought. But she squared her shoulders in an unconscious gesture, bent her lips into a semblance of a smile, and nodded affirmatively at her father.

Joanne O'Connor was talking nonstop as the three walked toward the building. "I feel better already. Once we've had a chance to talk to Willard Pugh face to face and explain the extent of your involvement, he'll lift your suspension. I'm certain of that. I mean, you're hardly an incorrigible student. And it's not as if you aren't going to be punished. You've already spent a night in jail, and you've still got a court date. . . .I mean, if they're going to suspend you, they should look to all the others who were there and just didn't get caught, and do the same to them."

Beth was aghast. "Mother! Please! Just let me explain everything. When I'm finished I'm sure he'll just give me a few detentions, and the whole thing will be over with. I wish you didn't have to be here at all."

Beth immediately regretted the last remark, but it was too late to retract it. Her father's hand came down on her shoulder, forcing her to stop walking. "That's enough, Beth. Neither your mother nor I want to be here, can't you understand that? I didn't want to be at the police station last night, either. But I was summoned there, and she and I were summoned here, as a direct result, I might add, of some rather unfortunate actions of yours, young lady. Remember that. Now let's go face the music."

They had reached the heavy double doors that led into the building, and Mr. O'Connor held open the right one for his wife and daughter. They threaded their way through the halls and toward Mr. Pugh's office. Beth knew they were an odd procession. No one came to school with their parents—not both of them, anyway. A few students greeted her, and she returned their "Hi's" with what she hoped was a casual "Hi" of her own. Others, however, avoided her eyes and pretended to be engrossed in conversation as they passed her by—but not before Beth saw their eyes locking on her face, then quickly pulling away. People knew what had happened last night. And everyone was talking.

Joanne O'Connor had regained her composure.

"Look!" she said. "There's Martha. I want to talk to her for just a minute."

Martha was in the middle of a knot of students waiting to enter the chemistry lab. She was laughing and talking to Marie Arcola, gesturing with her hands, the way she always did when she was excited. When she looked up and saw the O'Connors moving toward her, she took all of them in with a glance and greeted them with a wave and a sympathetic smile.

Beth caught Martha's eye and shook her head from side to side, almost imperceptibly, willing her friend to disappear into the safety of the chemistry lab, away from her mother's interrogation. Martha caught the signal, flashed an even brighter smile, then pulled Marie into the lab with her.

"You're too late, Mother," Beth said with relief. The warning bell rang and the door to the chemistry lab closed. It was one-thirty, time for the meeting with Willard Pugh.

Mr. Pugh's secretary, a birdlike woman whose stockings bagged at the ankles, greeted the O'Connors nervously. She offered them coffee, and when they refused, she returned to her desk where she pushed papers around and made soft clucking sounds as she worked. She seemed unwilling to look Beth in the face. Within a minute, the intercom on her desk buzzed, and she stood up and smoothed her skirt. "Mr. Pugh is ready to see you now," was all she said.

The principal's manner was cordial, even friendly, when the O'Connors entered his office. He jumped up from behind his massive desk. "Hello there. I'm

Willard Pugh," he said, shoving a fat hand toward Beth's father, who shook it and merely said, "Franklin O'Connor." Mr. Pugh seemed to expect something more. "Yes," he said, and cleared his throat unnecessarily. He gestured them into chairs which had been pulled up in front of the desk. Then he turned to Joanne. "Well now, it's surely good to see you again, Mrs. O'Connor. Surely is. It was a lot more pleasant the last time, wasn't it? Cultural Arts Fair doings, I believe. Well, well, well. These kiddos and football season. What are we going to do with them?" He gave a little conspiratorial smile to both Franklin and Joanne, then shook his head at Beth.

"Apparently, arrest them," Joanne O'Connor snapped. The words echoed uncomfortably around the room.

Beth threw what she hoped was an imploring look at her mother and sank lower into her seat. She saw Mr. Pugh stiffen, and the smile faded from his face. He faced Joanne steadily and said, "Well, they were trespassing, you know."

Joanne replied evenly and reasonably. "So is every parent who plays tennis on the school courts on Saturday afternoon."

"Well now, we're not talking about tennis here, are we? We're talking vandalism, and vandalism is a serious offense, believe you me. Vandalism calls for suspension—it says so right in the book."

"What book?" Franklin O'Connor asked.

"Why, the policy book of the school district." Mr. Pugh tapped a thick volume that he had laid conspicuously on the corner of his desk. "You can look it up for yourself—it's under 'Discipline': *Vandalism is the willful destruction of school property.* There was thousands of dollars worth of damage done to that school. I've never seen Earl Harper as mad as he was last night, and I can't blame him. Can't blame him at all." Then, turning to Beth, he said, "You have anything you want to tell me, girl? Can you explain any of this? We haven't heard a word from you."

Beth swallowed hard. Her mother's words echoed in her brain: . . . *no need to mention the car unless you're asked . . . don't have to testify against yourself.* "I promise, Mr. Pugh, I didn't do any thousand dollars' worth of damage. You know me. I wouldn't hurt Woodrow; I wouldn't hurt any school deliberately. But what about them? They stole our cougar, right from this building in broad daylight. All we wanted to do was get it back. I'm sorry, Mr. Pugh, really sorry I went over there. I didn't know anything like this could happen. Everybody has done this kind of thing for years. It's football tradition. I never dreamed we could get into this kind of trouble." Beth said it all in a rush, not stopping to draw a breath. Now, when she inhaled, her lungs expanded jerkily, and the sound of her breathing filled the office.

Willard Pugh rocked slowly in his chair while she talked. When Beth finished, he took a sharpened pencil from a cup that said "World's Best Dad" and began tapping it aimlessly on a pad of paper on his desk. "Beth, I've got two points I want to make with you right now." He drew a 1 with a circle around it on the pad. "Right after the pep rally I began to hear rumors that some of you seniors were fixing to—I believe you called it 'liberate'—the cougar. Now, as soon as I got wind of that, I told Coach Killough and the entire faculty to buttonhole you kids one by one, if necessary, and tell you what would happen if any of you got caught over at Woodrow. Fact is, just yesterday afternoon I personally sat Miss Martha Worley right down in that chair and I told her that anybody caught at Woodrow would get suspension. She's a mighty close friend of yours. Don't ask me to believe she didn't tell you about our little chat. So your story won't float my boat. No, ma'am, it won't."

Beth sat in stunned silence for a moment. So Martha had known exactly what could happen all along. Her mouth felt stiff when she began to talk. "She didn't say anything to me, Mr. Pugh. I promise. I'd heard the football team had been warned, but nobody said a word about the rest of us. This kind of thing goes on every year, you know that. And anyway, at the pep rally you said we'd get our cougar back—we just wanted to be sure we had it before the game, that's all."

Joanne O'Connor said, "Mr. Pugh, surely it's unfair that some children were warned and others weren't . . ."

The principal reached in his pocket for a handkerchief and blew his nose into it heartily, stopping Joanne in mid-sentence. "They were all warned as far as I'm concerned," he said flatly. "And as far as getting the cougar back, I surely wasn't condoning vandalism at that pep rally, no sirree. Earl and I were just saying last night that this foolishness has gone on too long. It's embarrassing. Some of the things that were sprayed on Woodrow's walls . . . well, I haven't seen anything quite like that in . . . well, not since my days in the army. And speaking of paint, the police tell me you had green paint on your hands when they picked you up. You want to tell me anything about that? Doesn't seem to me it takes paint to get that cougar back." He drew a 2 and circled it, then leaned back in his chair and let the office fill with silence again.

Beth looked at her mother, then at her father. She thought she saw her father's head nod ever so slightly, but she couldn't be sure. The pulse in her throat was pounding. She rummaged in her purse and pulled out the handkerchief. Within a moment it was a damp wad in her hand.

Beth drew in a shaky breath and her voice quavered at first. "Mr. Pugh, I'll tell you the truth," she said. "I did paint a few words on the trunk of the vocational ed car over there . . . the one that sits outside the shop building. But Woodrow paints eagles on it all the time; then they refinish it. I didn't think it would hurt anything. That's all I did, I swear it on a stack of Bibles."

Before Beth could go on, Franklin O'Connor interrupted. "I'm prepared to pay to have that car professionally repainted, if that would satisfy everyone, Mr. Pugh. It seems like a fair offer to me."

Willard Pugh let his eyes slide slowly from Beth to her mother, then to her father. He touched the fingertips of his hands together and Beth stared at the huge gold nugget ring in the shape of Texas that he wore on his right hand. Please let him accept Dad's offer. Please, she prayed silently.

The principal pursed his lips. "The district will expect you to pay for those damages, naturally. Those and any other damages Beth is charged with."

At the look on Franklin O'Connor's face, Mr. Pugh held up a pudgy hand. "Now, now, don't go getting excited. I understand that Beth wasn't the only Millington student over at Woodrow last night. This was a well-planned escapade, and that brings me to my second point." Willard Pugh tapped the number 2 on his tablet. "I've heard that there was a planning meeting at Carl Loessing's house. You know anything about that, Beth? It would surely help us get this matter straightened out quickly if we knew everybody who was involved. A little lady like you couldn't possibly have done all that damage."

He twisted his chair suddenly to the right and looked directly at Beth, who felt her insides drop the way they did when she rode the Rocket at the State Fair. She sat silently, staring at Mr. Pugh, who tried again.

"Now, Beth, I can't promise anything, but well, ahhhh, it could be that your punishment will be lighter if we could find out exactly who else was over at Woodrow the other night. Why don't you be a good girl and help us out? You know you and Carl would feel better if you weren't the only ones taking the blame."

"I thought three students were arrested," Joanne O'Connor interrupted. "Wasn't John Bartlett taken in, too?"

"John's not the subject of this conversation," Willard Pugh said sharply. "It would be inappropriate for me to discuss one student with another student's parents. Surely you understand, Mrs. O'Connor." He shifted his attention back to Beth. "Well, Beth?" he said.

"I really don't have anything more to say," she answered. Her voice was barely a whisper.

Willard Pugh let out an enormous sigh and reached for a pink form that lay on a stack of similar forms placed to his left. All the blanks had been filled in, and Beth saw her name at the top. When Mr. Pugh handed the form to Beth, she saw Carl's name filled in on the one underneath. Mr. Pugh fished a pen out of his coffee cup and handed it to Beth. "You'll need to sign this on the bottom," he said.

"What is it?" Beth asked.

"It's your suspension notice. It's only for three days, and today counts as the first. After that, you'll be assigned to the I.S.C. for six weeks."

"The I.S.C.!" The letters came out of Beth's mouth in a kind of horror-struck whisper. To her knowledge, only one other person from Millington had ever been sent there—a boy who was caught selling drugs on the parking lot during lunch. He never returned to Millington. Everyone said he quit school permanently after serving just one week.

Joanne O'Connor looked at her husband, then at

Mr. Pugh. "I'm confused," she said. "What exactly is this I.S.C.?"

Willard Pugh ran his forefinger inside his shirt collar, as if it were suddenly choking him, and he cleared his throat before he spoke. "The letters stand for Incorrigible Student Center." The principal quickly held his hand up again to silence Beth's mother before she spoke. "Now, no one's saying Beth's incorrigible. This is a lot better than expelling Beth or suspending her for the entire semester."

"I've never heard of such a thing," Franklin O'Connor said. "Is it like detention? Is it here at Millington?"

Mr. Pugh looked uncomfortable again. "Well, no, it's not. It's in a separate facility across town. We can't have these students mingling with the general school population."

"I thought you just said Beth wasn't that kind of student," Joanne exclaimed.

"This meeting's taken up enough of my time, Mrs. O'Connor. Beth, you have to sign this." He pushed another form across the desk to her. "It's your transfer to the I.S.C."

Joanne O'Connor shot from her seat as if she had just received an electric shock. "She'll sign nothing of the kind! This is preposterous! Utterly ridiculous! I don't approve of what Beth's done, but I don't approve of your tactics, either, Mr. Pugh. You were at the jail Monday night, but you never even talked to Beth or saw that she'd called home. You didn't get the facts but you'd already made up your mind about Beth's guilt and her punishment. You even had the suspension and transfer forms filled out before we got here. Well, let me tell you, my daughter's not going to be the scapegoat for the entire student body."

"Mother, please . . ." Beth said miserably.

Mr. Pugh stood up. "You know, Mrs. O'Connor, I used to be a coach, and every once in a while I'd have to eat a tough call. This is a tough call for all of you, I know. But Beth'll bounce back. Winners always do, and I'm sure down deep inside, Beth's a winner. It is also my duty to inform you that you may appeal my decision to the superintendent of schools. Of course, she doesn't have to listen to your appeal, but you can try." The last sentences were said formally, as if they were all in court.

"I—we—will certainly be appealing," said Joanne, glancing at her husband for support.

"Well, I don't think it'll do much good, and it could cause Beth here some real embarrassment, hanging out all that dirty linen," the principal answered.

"I don't think Beth's linen is as dirty as some, Mr. Pugh," Joanne snapped as she headed toward the door.

The principal didn't answer, but Beth saw the muscles in his face harden. His words tumbled out of his mouth as if he were in a hurry to get them over with. "Go clean out your gym locker and your school locker and return your textbooks to my secretary. You're no longer a student here at Millington. As soon as your suspension is served, you'll report to the I.S.C. They'll issue you new books there."

CHAPTER

EIGHT

Beth woke the following morning with the vague feeling that something was wrong, although for her first moments of consciousness she couldn't put her finger on exactly what it was. In the next room, Ruthanne was slamming drawers as she got ready for school. School. That was it. She wasn't going to school today. Or tomorrow. She wouldn't be inside the halls of Millington for weeks. Beth rolled over and buried her face in her pillow, wishing she could sleep through all six of them. She didn't hear the door of her bedroom push open and paid no attention at all to the soft footsteps until a hot pink tongue began licking her hand.

"Go away, Barney," Beth said, still not opening her eyes as she gave the huge dog a push.

"Just because you've got problems is no excuse to take them out on a poor dog," said Ruthanne.

Beth's eyes popped open. "How long have you been here?" she said.

"Not long. I just came to say . . . to say good-bye. And I wondered if there's anything I'm supposed to tell people when they ask why you've been expelled from school." Ruthanne's voice was a mixture of anger with just a trace of pity.

"I haven't been expelled, I've been suspended. There's a difference. Why don't you just say 'no comment,' like the people in the news? You don't know anything, anyway." Beth didn't look at Ruthanne, but continued to stare at the wall.

"I know enough, and I can guess the rest," Ruthanne said. "You and those stupid Misses."

"Ruthie, get out of here, and take Barney with you. I have a headache."

Ruthanne stomped out of the room and slammed the door shut, leaving the dog in Beth's room. The slamming door made Barney jump onto the bed, but instead of pushing him away, Beth wrapped her arms around his considerable bulk. "What am I going to do, Barney old boy?" she whispered into his furry hide.

Beth couldn't go back to sleep, so she climbed out of bed and pulled a piece of notebook paper from her desk. She sat down and decisively wrote "Things to Do Today" across the top of it. Then she stared at the paper. It dawned on her sickeningly that there was nothing to list: no tests to prepare for, no papers to write, no meetings to attend. The Misses had had their monthly meeting last night—Mrs. Worley had reminded Beth of that fact when Beth had called and asked for Martha. Martha had never returned her call. Beth desperately wanted to know what was said at the meeting. She picked up her pen. "Talk to Martha TODAY!!!!" she wrote on her list.

The rest of the day crawled by. Mrs. O'Connor left at ten o'clock, reminding Beth that it was her volunteer day at the hospital and that she had planned a few errands for the afternoon. The house seemed strangely still. Beth flipped on the television, but she couldn't concentrate on watching anything, not even the soap operas. She marked the passage of each hour by how it would pass at school. Eleven o'clock. She'd be in English now. Twelve noon. It was lunch, a good time for Martha to call. But lunch came and went and the phone in the O'Connor house stayed silent. Finally, Beth remembered that Carl was probably suspended, too. It was worth calling his house to find out. She wasn't surprised when he picked up the phone after two rings.

"Hi. What's going on?" It was her standard greeting, but now it had much more significance.

Carl's voice was dull. "Not much. Just sitting here."

"How much suspension did you get?" Beth asked.

"Till the end of the week."

"I only got three days. You going to the I.S.C. then? My parents are appealing my sentence."

There was a silence on the phone that lasted a millisecond too long. "I didn't get I.S.C. I just got four days of suspension."

Beth was shocked and angry. "Why not? You were arrested along with me."

"Yeah, but I didn't have any paint on my hands, kid. There was nothing to tie me to any of the damage. Anyway, you should relax. You said you were going to appeal. You'll get out of the I.S.C. Only druggies go there."

Beth swallowed hard. "Do you know what happened to John?"

"Not yet," Carl answered. "He was suspended yesterday, but he's up there with his father right now, talking to Pugh. He's in for it, though. The football players knew what would happen if they tried anything."

"Did you know what would happen, Carl?"

"I had an idea," he answered.

"I swear I didn't. Nothing like this has ever happened before."

"I know," Carl said disgustedly. "Did you know old man Harper isn't even trying to find out who stole our cougar?" Carl's voice was rising in anger. "Whoever did that started this whole mess," he added bitterly.

The call-waiting button clicked on Beth's phone, and she terminated her conversation with Carl. It was her father calling from the bank to see how she was. She assured him she was all right, just bored. When that conversation ended, Beth wandered into her sister's room and studied the pictures of Dunney that were tacked on Ruthanne's bulletin board. With a shock Beth realized that she was even looking forward to seeing Ruthie when she got home from school.

Finally, at four o'clock, the phone rang again, and Beth grabbed it eagerly.

"Hi, it's Jed."

Beth's heart was thumping—she could feel it high in her chest—and those funny, rippling feelings were running up and down inside. Please, God, she prayed, let my voice sound normal. "Jed! I'm so glad you called. How are you?"

"Okay. I really ought to be asking you that question."

"I'm fine." The automatic answer came out right on cue, and Beth was glad it did. "How was school?" She could feel her throat close at the thought of Millington, and she picked up a pencil and began to doodle large *M*'s on the notepad that sat by the telephone.

"Not so red hot. John's parents are having a fit about him not playing Saturday night. Pugh told the Bartletts that they'd probably feel better if all of the kids who were at Woodrow got punished. Then he tried to force John to give him a list of names. Can you believe it? It's Gestapo tactics."

"Yeah, I can believe it," Beth said, remembering Mr. Pugh's offer of leniency if she would cooperate.

"Anyway, I can't believe he kicked John off the team, what with the game coming up and all. I've gotta have him—he's my only reliable receiver. My dad's gonna talk to him, though, and—you know—try to straighten him out."

"Mr. Pugh, or John?" Beth asked.

"Pugh, of course. John doesn't need straightening out. What he needs is to be on the team, if we're going to win Saturday."

"Sorry . . . it was a stupid question." The sharpened point of the pencil she was holding snapped off, and Beth was surprised to see that the *M*'s she had been tracing and retracing had gone through the top page of the tablet. With a jolt, she realized that she wouldn't be able to attend the game at all. Suspended students and students at the I.S.C. were expressly forbidden to set foot on any property that belonged to the school district. That information was in bold black letters on the bottom of Beth's transfer to the I.S.C. and her suspension notice.

Jed, unaware of Beth's thoughts, chatted on. "It's not a dumb question," he said amiably. "Girls just don't understand the crucial way a football team is balanced. Uh, listen, Beth. I really need to talk to you. Can I come over? Maybe pick you up, and we'll go for a Coke or something?"

She tried to make her tone casual as she said, "Oh, sure, that'll be just fine."

Within ten minutes two short blasts of the horn announced the arrival of Jed and his Bronco. Beth scribbled a note to her mother, hurried outside, and climbed up into the seat next to Jed. They drove to a nearby Baskin-Robbins and got double-dip cones, then headed to a small park at the edge of Beth's neighborhood to eat them.

Jed parked the truck under the shade of a giant oak. "Oh, man, would you look at that?" he said, sounding as if he had just seen the newest Mazda RX7. He pointed toward a group of trees about a hundred yards away. Crude human figures wearing football jerseys were hanging by the neck from the branches. "WE," for Woodrow Eagles, had been sprayed in yellow paint across their chests.

"I heard some of the guys were going to do that when the cougar was stolen, but I was afraid they hadn't gotten around to it, what with all the trouble with Pugh and everything," Jed said as he and Beth walked toward them. Jed tugged at one of the figures, and a wad of crumpled tissue paper stuffing fell to the ground. "Uh oh. I broke his leg," Jed said, smiling.

A few yards away, in another group of trees, more figures hung. These had "MC" sprayed on them. Beth walked over to them and stared upward. "It looks like Woodrow's out for blood, too," she said as she looked at the Millington effigies, swaying crazily in the gentle breeze.

"Sure they are," Jed answered. "Just like us."

Something about the dancing figures chilled Beth, but she decided to remain silent. Broken green peppers and smashed tomatoes littered the ground. Beth pushed some of the decaying vegetables away with her foot. "It seems like such a waste of good food," she said, and hated herself for sounding like her mother.

"That's just the casualties of the tomato and pepper war," Jed said cheerfully.

Beth stole a quick glance at him. He still hadn't told her what he wanted to talk about. Jed picked up a green pepper that had somehow managed to remain intact. He pulled his arm back as if he were throwing a football and aimed it at the face of a Woodrow figure hanging nearby. The pepper cracked when it hit, and left seeds on the face of the effigy. "Bull's-eye," Jed said with satisfaction. "Man, we are not only famous, we are getting to be positively notorious. This game's got everybody in town revved up. Did you see Oscar Britton's editorial in the *Tribune* this morning?"

Beth took the last bite of her ice cream cone and she shook her head. "My family takes the *Daily News*. What'd he say?"

"Oh, he started out about the cheerleaders. You know, Angela's head cheerleader this year."

Beth nodded. Everyone at Millington knew Angela Britton and knew that her father was the editor of Fort Preston's evening paper.

"Well, he started off by saying that Millington had the best cheerleaders in the state of Texas, and that they were going to help us win Saturday night's game, hands down. Oh, and he gave you a plug, too."

"He did?" Beth was amazed that Oscar Britton, who usually wrote conservative columns about government spending and illegal aliens, would bother to write anything about high school football. She tugged on Jed's arm. "Well, go on. What did he say?"

Jed was smiling now, enjoying her anticipation. "Man, you should have seen it. It's been Xeroxed and put on all the bulletin boards at school. At least, it's on the coaches' bulletin boards. What'll you give me if I tell you?" he said.

"What do you want?" she answered, then blushed violently at the thought of how that comment could be interpreted. A breeze blew the scent of Jed's after-shave toward her, and she busied herself picking a piece of imaginary lint off her sweater. Why did she have to be so aware of his physical presence? It made her say things she didn't really want to say, think things she really didn't want to think.

"I'll tell you what Oscar Britton said now, and I'll collect on what I want later." Jed raised his eyebrows in a lecherous Groucho Marx imitation that made Beth laugh. "He said that the Millington Cougars had two things going for them in Saturday night's game—the finest cheerleaders in Texas, and the fact that a few members of its student body had gone over to Woodrow and thoroughly trashed up the place. What do you think of that?"

Jed looked pleased with himself, and Beth got the distinct impression that, had she been a guy, he would have punched her in the arm or slapped her on the fanny in his exuberance. As for her, hearing what was in the evening paper made her heart sink.

"What do I think?" she cried. "I think it's, it's . . . terrible. I can't believe he said that—in the paper, of all places! I didn't 'thoroughly trash up' the place. And lots of kids were there, not 'a few members of the student body.' Where's he getting his information? He's supposed to be a journalist, interested in facts. Did he mention my name? I'll die if he did. I'll die, right now." Her heart slammed against her rib cage. She jumped off the picnic table where she and Jed were sitting and began to pace back and forth in front of him. She thought of her mother's reaction when she read the piece in the paper, for surely one of Joanne's friends would see to it that she got a copy. She shuddered and pushed the thought of her mother out of her mind.

Jed hopped down after her and caught her by the shoulders, slowing her down. "Whoaa. Don't get so excited. He just meant that this would be a good contest—a kind of grudge match. You know. And you guys provided the grudge."

"Woodrow stole our mascot!"

"That's what he means. In the past Woodrow's painted us up. Then they stole our mascot, so we trashed them up. Now both sides want to get even on the football field. Man, it's going to be a great game. Calm down, it's not like he mentioned your name or anything. And even if he did, well, you did it all for dear old alma mater and the Cougars."

Jed was still holding her, and Beth made no effort to move. He looked at her directly and said, "And besides, you were there, you know."

"I know," she said quietly.

They were walking across the park now, in an aimless kind of stroll. Jed let one arm drape across Beth's shoulders, and she, in turn, put an arm around his waist, threading a finger through a belt loop on his jeans. She was certain she could discern the movement of every muscle in his body as they walked, and she wondered if that could be possible. They continued in silence for a while, each lost in private thoughts. Finally, Jed cleared his throat, and pulled Beth down next to him on a park bench.

"You look good in that color," he said. He was still holding her hand, and her body was doing funny things to her head. She managed a smile and a low-voiced "thank you." He was so close now that she could see the little flecks of color in his eyes. They weren't entirely blue as she had thought. They had gray in them, too.

"Beth," he said, "I need to talk to you."

Overhead, two squirrels scolded and chased each other through the boughs of an oak tree, making a Millington effigy jerk crazily on the end of its string. He squeezed her hand, then dropped it and wiped the palms of his hands on the knees of his jeans.

"Beth, you're not going to tell Pugh who else was over at Woodrow, are you?"

She was shocked by the abrupt change in the tone in his voice, but he hurried on before she had a chance to respond.

"I mean, some of the guys on the team are pretty worried. Everybody's got to be eligible to play if we're going to win Saturday night. We can't go out there with a bunch of bench-warmers and expect to beat Woodrow. Not that the whole gang isn't behind you, understand. We think it stinks—what's happened to you and John and Carl."

"I just found out what happened to Carl this afternoon. How does everybody know so much?" Beth didn't like the idea of others knowing more about this situation than she did.

"Relax. I'm not spying on you. Pugh got on the P.A. and announced your punishments."

Beth was astonished. "When did he do that?" she asked.

"Yesterday morning, Babe, before you ever got to school."

No wonder everybody had looked like such scared rabbits when she and her parents had arrived, Beth thought. No wonder no one looked her in the eye—no one but Martha.

"Now, like I said, my dad's going to try to get Mr. Pugh to let John play, but that may not work. And we can't lose anybody else. We just can't have any football players' names being brought to Pugh's attention. Do you know what I mean?" He spoke hurriedly, as if he couldn't stand the taste of the words while they were in his mouth.

Beth flinched as if she had taken a physical blow. The ice cream cone rolled and tossed dangerously in her stomach. Instinctively, she reached over and touched Jed on his knee—she couldn't be sure whether the gesture was intended to reassure him, or herself. When she pulled her hand back, the rough texture of the denim lingered on her fingertips. "I . . . I think I know what you mean. I wasn't going to say anything, Jed. I really wasn't. But aren't you worried about Carl, or John, or any of the others talking? I mean, why is everybody so worried about me and what I'll say? There were lots of other kids there that night."

Jed looked uncomfortable. "Well, my dad saw your mom at the administration building earlier today. He was going over the agenda for Monday's school board meeting, and she walked out of Dr. Dycus's office. He said she looked feisty, mighty feisty." Jed laughed in an indulgent way, as if women who were "feisty" were somehow cute. "My dad says we can't have anybody else stirring this pot."

Beth nodded, although she wasn't sure what he was asking of her.

"I told him you were a team player from the word go. Always have been. But he thinks your mom's considering suing the school or something because of what happened to you."

Beth's heart sank. "Suing the school? Don't be crazy! She . . . she can't do anything like that. Not without me. I'm sure she just wanted to talk to Dr. Dycus. Mr. Pugh said we could appeal to her—maybe that's what she was doing. She doesn't want me to have to go to the I.S.C., Jed. I don't want to go there, either. I'm terrified. It's a place for criminals."

"You won't be there long, sweetheart," Jed said soothingly. "My father'll get you out in no time. Your mom's just gotta play it cool, that's all. No waves. The Bartletts are cooling it, too. Dad says Pugh backed himself into a corner after he shot his mouth off on the P.A. system, so we've got to lighten up or he'll never be able to back off his punishments. This game's too important to risk upsetting any more people."

Beth took Jed's hand and looked at him directly. "I swear to you, Jed, I won't let Mother make any waves."

"That's great. I just sort of promised the guys I'd . . . well, I promised them I'd . . . well, talk to you, you know?"

"Yeah, I know," Beth said.

"And another thing—I'm sorry about the game and the dance."

"The dance?" Beth asked stupidly.

"Yeah, well, you know. You and I were going to go together and all that. I mean, now you can't what with the suspension and all."

Beth hadn't even thought about the dance after Saturday's game, but she knew instantly that what Jed said was true. The dance was a school-sponsored event. She was barred from attending that, too.

"Who are you going to take?" she asked.

"Probably nobody. It's a little late to be asking, don't you think? I'll just show up stag."

Jed was holding her hand again, leading her back toward the parked Bronco. He was whistling under his breath, and seemed relaxed now that he had gotten through this conversation.

The truck edged its way through the late-afternoon traffic. Dozens of cars from Millington clogged Washington Drive. They were easy to spot. Ribbons of green and black crepe paper flew from radio antennas and door handles. Messages from the Misses, similar to the ones she and Martha had left at Jed's house on Sunday night, were written in white shoe polish across the windows of the football players' cars. In some cases, the drivers could barely see. Jed stopped at a red light, and a station wagon pulled up next to them. Martha honked the horn, and Jed lowered his window to lean out and talk to her.

"Your car's too clean! Where have you been? We need to get you fixed up." At that moment, Martha and Beth saw each other. Beth wondered if it was her imagination, or did Martha's smile fade a little when she saw who was in the Bronco with Jed?

"Beth!" she exclaimed. "I've been meaning to call you. How's it going? Lord, I wish I had a few days off," she said with a laugh.

The light turned green then, and both station wagon and truck pulled away from the intersection. Martha gave two toots on the horn and waved her arm as she turned left.

Within a minute, they had arrived at Beth's house. "If you wanted to wait, I could decorate the Bronco for you. I think I still have some of my supplies," she said.

Jed looked surprised at the offer. "I don't know. I don't think I'd risk it if I were you. Old Pugh might call it vandalism, you know." He was smiling down at her now, and the two of them had walked up to the front porch.

The voice bursting out of Beth didn't sound like her own, it was so high-pitched and shrill. "I don't know what's vandalism and what isn't anymore. It isn't vandalism to steal a mascot. It isn't vandalism to throw vegetables in the park. It isn't vandalism if Woodrow paints up our school. It certainly isn't vandalism if we paint up our driveways—the art departments make our stupid stencils! But it sure is vandalism if I paint on the trunk of the vocational ed car." Beth thought of Martha. "Or maybe it's just vandalism if you get caught," she added bitterly.

Jed looked at her peculiarly. "Calm down," he said.

Beth was breathing hard and fighting tears. "Oh,

Jed, this is so hard, you know? It's awful, not being allowed to be a part of anything. I mean, I can't even go to school! Everybody moans about school all the time, but to not be allowed to go . . . you just can't imagine how that feels—it feels like . . . like I'm walking around without my skin on. I know that sounds stupid, but it's true. You really can't imagine what suspension feels like. And the I.S.C.—it's going to be like the jail was, I know it will."

Jed looked uncomfortable. "I told you. That's not gonna happen. And even if it does, it won't be for long. Dad says it's no place for a girl like you." In an elaborate gesture, he looked at his watch. "Gosh, it's five-thirty—I've got to get a move on. A recruiter from U.T. is taking Mom and Dad and me to dinner. There could be a scholarship in it. I'll catch you later."

Beth nodded and watched from the entrance hall as his Bronco pulled away. She knew Martha, and possibly a horde of Misses, would be waiting at Jed's house when he got home. Adelaide Stuart, dressed for her dinner with the University of Texas recruiter, would be plying the girls with soft drinks, candy, and assurances that Jed would be home "any minute now." While he and his parents were at dinner, Beth knew the Misses would turn Jed's Bronco into something that resembled a float in the Cotton Bowl parade.

CHAPTER

NINE

By Thursday, Beth wondered if she was getting sick. She had no fever, but her body felt sluggish, and she dragged herself from room to room wondering how she was going to get through another interminable day. The desperation of total and complete boredom might have driven her to studying, but she had no textbooks and wouldn't get any until she entered the I.S.C. the next day.

Her aimless travels took her into the den, where she found her mother leafing through the Millington High School student handbook. Students were issued a copy at the beginning of each school year. They were expected to sign and return a card to the school indicating that they had read it. Beth had dutifully read through the rules and regulations the first two years at Millington, but since nothing ever changed, now she just signed the card and returned it, stacking the past two years' handbooks on top of the others on the bottom shelf of her bookcase.

"What are you doing with the handbook?" Beth asked.

"I'm trying to find out how this school district is run. I went over to the administration building yesterday to see if I could borrow a copy of that policy book that Mr. Pugh kept referring to, but I didn't have any luck. Helen Dycus's secretary said Dr. Dycus was out of town and she refused to lend me a copy without her permission." Joanne O'Connor laughed slightly. "I'm afraid I behaved badly. Poor woman—it's not her fault, but I threatened to sue under the Texas Open Records Act to get a copy of the book. It didn't do any good, but I did get all of us an appointment to see Dr. Dycus at ten o'clock on Monday, so I accomplished something."

Beth felt relieved. Jed's father had probably overheard this exchange, which is why he thought her mother might sue. Well, her mother was definitely not going to sue over a dumb policy book, that much was certain.

"Anyway, I grabbed this handbook from Ruthanne's room. It's this year's copy and I wanted to see what it says about suspension and vandalism and the I.S.C., but I've just found something much more interesting."

She opened the book to the section on discipline,

110

and Beth saw that her mother had used a yellow highlighter on the subsection titled "Jurisdiction of the School." Joanne adjusted her glasses on the tip of her nose. "Listen to this," she said, and began to read aloud. " 'The school shall have jurisdiction over its students for discipline purposes from the time of departure from home until arrival at home at the close of the school day. Misconduct *during this time*' "— Joanne emphasized the last three words—" 'becomes a matter of *school discipline*' "—more emphasis on the last two—" 'if the interest of the school is involved.' " Joanne closed the handbook with a flourish. "I think we can use this technicality with Dr. Dycus if reason doesn't work."

"I don't understand," Beth said. "We were on their property."

"Absolutely. And they had the right to call the police and press charges, just like any property owner. But they don't have the right to punish you with suspension and the I.S.C. You and the others were at Woodrow around nine at night. You weren't misbehaving on their time. They tell us what they consider to be 'their' time, right here in this student handbook, which each student *has* to read." Joanne O'Connor picked the book up and handed it to Beth. "Read it for yourself," she said.

Beth glanced over the section, but didn't read it. There was no need. Joanne O'Connor wouldn't have made a mistake. Still, it surprised Beth that her mother was looking for technicalities and loopholes like this. In the past, Beth and Ruthanne had always been told, "If you get in trouble at school, you'll be in double trouble at home."

The phone rang, interrupting Beth's thoughts. She bolted from the sofa to catch it, then stopped. Who would be calling her at ten o'clock on a school-day morning? Her mother answered it, then handed the receiver to Beth. "Well, well, well," she whispered. "It's long-lost Martha."

"I'll get it in my room," Beth answered. Once there, she closed the door and picked up the receiver. "Hello?"

"I don't have much time—I'm calling from the coach's office," Martha said. "I just wanted to know how you were. Sorry I haven't returned your call before now. Things have been pretty wild around here, but I guess you know that."

"There are some things I just found out, Martha, and other things I need to know. That's why I called you. Jed says everybody at school is running scared."

"Not *everybody*," Martha corrected. "It's all John Bartlett's fault. Or his parents', to be precise. They're mad because he got suspended and can't play on Saturday night. They want everybody who was at Woodrow searched out and destroyed, so to speak, and I told you how Pugh reacts to parents complaining, remember?" Beth remembered. She thought of her mother; Joanne O'Connor would probably agree with the Bartletts. "Anyway, Jed's calming everybody down today. He thinks John may get to play, after all—his dad's going to try to reason with Pugh. And, Beth, Jed said the nicest things about you."

"He did? What?" Beth's heart lifted for the first time that day.

"Well, he just reassured all of us that you're a team player. That's what he called you—'a team player.' Coming from him, that's a high compliment. You really won't say anything about . . . well, about who was at Woodrow, will you?"

Beth's spirits plummeted, pushing away any warmth she still felt for her friend. "Now you listen to me," she began. "I am so sick of defending myself over and over on that point that I could scream. No! For the last time! I'm not going to squeal, okay? But while we're on the subject of who betrays whom, Martha Worley, how come you didn't tell me what would happen if we got caught?"

"You knew the football team would get in trouble," Martha said indignantly.

"Yeah, but Mr. Pugh said he told you *specifically* that anybody who went to Woodrow would be suspended. And then, right there in Carl's driveway, we talked about the mascots and you never said a word about your precious warning. You only mentioned the team."

"Beth, you are such a wuss!! We were already into it by then. And I didn't think Pugh's warning meant a thing. We all get warned about lots of stuff, and we still do it. Besides, nobody hog-tied you and dragged you there. You're just mad because you got caught."

"Well, I wouldn't have gone if I'd had a warning. I think you knew that, and that's why you didn't say anything."

"What a wuss!" Martha said again, and this time she let the word hiss. Then, abruptly, she said, "I've got to go," and the receiver went dead.

Beth sat on her bed and held the phone in her hand until a warning beep made her replace it. Having it out with Martha hadn't made her feel much better.

There was a rap on her bedroom door, then her mother came into the room. "What did Martha have to say?" she asked.

"She says John may get to play football. Jed's father's working on it." Beth held her breath. She was waiting for her mother to explode at the injustice of it all. Instead, Joanne O'Connor frowned. "I can't believe that, Beth. It wouldn't be right—letting John play, while the rest of you are punished. I imagine it's just a rumor."

Beth, happy that her mother hadn't flown off the handle at the news, nodded her head. "Probably" is all she said in reply.

"Well, I have a busy day ahead of me," Joanne O'Connor said. She glanced at Beth, who hadn't bothered to change out of her nightclothes. "Will you be all right by yourself?" she asked.

"Mother! I'm seventeen years old!"

Mrs. O'Connor walked over to Beth and gave her a hug. "You're still my little girl, and I hate seeing you so unhappy. Get a bath and get dressed. You'll feel better. I'll be home by four." She disappeared, leaving a trail of Arpege perfume in her wake.

Beth did as her mother suggested and was vaguely surprised to see that she was right. She did feel better.

She grabbed an apple from its bowl on the kitchen counter, munching on it as she flipped on the television in the den. A toothy game show host was asking couples ridiculous questions about their married life, and Beth watched, amazed that adults would put themselves in these embarrassing circumstances just to win a refrigerator or a television. The host was saying, "Now, Ralph, will Debbie say . . ." when the phone rang. Beth cut off the television and raced to pick up the receiver.

"May I speak to Mrs. O'Connor, please?"

Beth recognized the voice instantly. "She isn't here right now. I don't know when she'll be back. Is this Mr. Pugh?"

"Well, then, Beth. Yes. Yes, it is." For some reason, the principal sounded embarrassed. "Do you happen to know where she's, uh, gone?" He tried to sound casual now, as if he always talked to Beth at home during the middle of a school day. When Beth indicated that she had no idea where her mother was, Willard Pugh seemed to make up his mind about something. His tone of voice changed and became hearty and enthusiastic, as if he was at the end of a pep rally.

"Well, now, Bethany, I might as well tell you the good news, since it concerns you and some of your friends and the matter of your behavior the other night. I've, uh, talked to some people, and, as it says in the Good Book, we sat down and reasoned together. Now, you know I don't hold with vandalism, and this situation certainly got out of hand. The perpetrators will have to be punished. But no one in this district is interested in giving you children"—Beth cringed at his use of "children"—"criminal records, so, uh, I believe that the district is prepared to drop those criminal charges. Provided, of course, that your parents pay for the damages that were done to Woodrow. How's that suit you, young lady?"

Beth sucked in her breath. "Do I still have to go to the I.S.C.?" she asked.

On the other end of the line the silence lasted a beat too long. "I've already made my decision, Bethany, and you know what it was. As I said, the perpetrators will have to be punished. I also told you that you can appeal to Dr. Dycus."

"But I'm going tomorrow!" Beth cried. "And Dr. Dycus can't see us until Monday."

"I can't help that, now, can I? Just have your mother or father call me, hear?"

"I will," Beth said, and she hung up the phone. So she wouldn't be going to court. They were going to drop the criminal charges. Relief began to come, slowly at first, then faster as the muscles in her neck and shoulders relaxed. Until this moment she hadn't realized how frightened she'd been at the thought of oaths and judges and the witness stand. She called her father immediately.

The happiness, mixed with relief, in his voice shocked Beth—wrapped up in her own concerns, she hadn't realized how worried he had been. "Are you sure, Beth? You're certain Mr. Pugh said that? That's wonderful. Tell your mother I'll take everyone out to dinner—we'll celebrate—just as long as you choose a reasonable place."

Beth's own spirits lifted as she listened to her father. Things were beginning to fall into place after all. No trial, and surely Dr. Dycus—with a little persuasion from Jed's father and her mother's argument about jurisdiction—would reduce her sentence to the I.S.C. Beth called Carl at home.

Mr. Pugh had not called the Loessings yet, so Beth broke the news about the district dropping the criminal charges. Carl's old bravado was back in place. "I knew they couldn't make anything stick. I'd just as soon have taken them on in court," he said.

"Well, I wouldn't," Beth said decisively. "We're still going to have to pay for the damages to Woodrow; that's why I'm calling. Didn't you say it cost five hundred dollars to repaint your whole car? How much do you think it would cost to just repaint a trunk?"

"It's not going to cost me anything," Carl said angrily. "I didn't do it."

Beth's heart sank. It was true. Carl hadn't painted on the car. Neither had John. She might have to stand the entire cost by herself.

"Listen, Beth," Carl was saying. "The kids in shop will repaint that car, so don't let the district stick you with a bunch of charges. I wouldn't give them a nickel over three hundred dollars if it were me. Anyway, Clara old girl, we've been avenged, rest assured. This cougar has pounced and pounced hard."

Adrenaline shot through Beth, and her heart beat in her throat. "Did you get the cougar back?"

"No," Carl answered disgustedly. "They've got it stashed somewhere where the sun don't shine. That's not what I'm talking about. It's almost better than that."

"Carl! Isn't everybody in enough trouble? It's not worth it. Whatever you did, go undo it."

"Too late, Babe. The deed is done. I gotta go—and remember this—Go Coogs!" With that final comment, Carl got off the phone.

Fresh anxiety diluted the relief that Beth had felt when she finished talking to Mr. Pugh, but she pushed it away. Whatever Carl had done—it had nothing to do with her. The problem at hand was earning enough money to pay for repainting the vocational ed car. She'd go to Fanner's today and apply for a job.

Fanner's department store was the most popular one in Fort Preston. "If you can't find it at Fanner's, forget it," its advertisements said, and it was true. The racks were crammed with new fall merchandise, but Beth ignored the tempting displays. She was looking for a salesperson or anyone connected with the store who could give her directions to the personnel department. It was lunchtime, and most of the departments were understaffed. Across the aisle, in junior sportswear, Beth heard the whir of a cash register. A group of mannequins dressed in jogging clothes blocked her view, but she knew that where a cash register sounded, a sales clerk was not far away. She headed in that direction.

"Well, I don't know. Do you think this will be all right for the dance?"

"I don't think John will care what you've got

on—he'll just be concentrating on trying to get it off."

"Martha Worley! Cut out your tongue! Anyway, if he doesn't get his suspension lifted he won't be playing *or* taking me to the dance."

Beth stopped short, almost running into the white plaster hand of one of the mannequins. What were Martha and Susan doing here? They were supposed to be in school. For a moment, she considered slipping away, but her feet refused to move. And anyway, they'd see her as soon as they finished making their purchases. Beth decided to be the first one to speak.

"Well, I thought I recognized a familiar voice," she said as she moved toward the two girls. Susan's face froze when she saw Beth, but Martha spoke first.

"What are you doing here?"

"I could ask you the same thing," Beth said evenly. "I thought we weren't supposed to leave campus for lunch."

"You know Fanny," said Martha, laughing lightly. "I'm bringing home the bacon—this time a bacon double cheeseburger."

"Well, suspension can't be that bad. Look at you— out shopping for the afternoon." Beth felt her smile freeze, then begin to melt from her face at the tone in Susan's voice.

"Not that I owe you an explanation, Susan, but I'm not shopping—I'm applying for a job. I'm going to have to pay for some of the damage that was done to Woodrow. I'll be sure to let you know what your share is."

"My share? Don't be crazy! I'm not paying a cent. Nobody's accused me of anything—at least, not yet.

But that's no thanks to you, now that your mother complained."

"That's enough, Susan," Martha said. "It's not Beth's mother who complained."

Beth's legs felt funny, and the blood made a roaring sound in her ears. She wanted to slap Susan—hard. She wanted to lash out at Martha, too. She didn't need anyone defending her or her mother. Beth's eyes moved from Susan's sour face to Martha's more sympathetic one. "I've got to go to personnel," she said quickly, "but I'll talk to both of you later. Be thinking about the money for the damages. That goes for you, too, Martha," Beth said as she walked away.

The personnel manager at Fanner's told Beth the store wasn't hiring at this time, but she was welcome to fill out an application and leave it on file. Somehow, she hadn't prepared herself for this possibility—she had assumed a job would be waiting for her as soon as she applied. Plenty of kids had worked at Fanner's over the summer. "The economy, you know," the personnel director had explained when Beth mentioned this fact. Beth accepted the application and sat in a desklike chair that reminded her of the ones at Millington. She began to fill out the application. When she came to the question, "Have you ever been arrested for anything other than a minor traffic violation? If so, explain on reverse side," she folded the application in half and explained to the personnel director that she was running late for a dental appointment and would bring it back later. When she was safely out of eyesight, she ripped it up and threw it in a trash can.

CHAPTER

TEN

It was pouring rain on Friday morning as Beth and her parents drove through Fort Preston to report to the I.S.C. The neighborhood that housed the facility was a crazy quilt made up of dilapidated frame houses with decaying living room furniture sitting on the front porches, pawnshops, junkyards, apartment buildings, and Taco Bells. No native pine trees softened the landscape in this neglected part of Fort Preston, home to transients, immigrants—legal and illegal—and the I.S.C.

Beth tried to ignore the scene outside the car window and instead stared at the raindrops as they beaded up, then flowed together down the glass. From the rear seat she could see the grim faces of her parents staring straight ahead. The car rolled to a stop in front of two large gates. A sign on one of them, simply lettered, said "Incorrigible Student Center, Valley Stream Independent School District." A six-foot chain link fence, topped by three strands of barbed wire, enclosed the facility, cutting it off from any contact with the neighborhood that surrounded it.

"It's eight-forty-five. We're ten minutes early. I don't know what we do now," Franklin O'Connor said, peering through the window at the closed gates. The windshield wipers made thumping sounds in the silence of the car.

"Well, I assume there won't be a footman to open the gates for us," Beth's mother answered. "This isn't a school . . . it's a prison. Look at it. They have bars on the windows."

It was true. There were bars on the windows and a grilled security gate across the front door.

"What kind of students need a place like this?" Beth's father asked.

"Incorrigible students, just like me, Dad," Beth answered bitterly.

"Some of them may need a place like this, but it ought to be a last resort, after everything else has been tried. You've never even had an overdue library book." Franklin O'Connor shook his head.

A buzzer sounded, and the electronically controlled gates swung open, obviously controlled from inside the building. The O'Connors' car drove through slowly, followed by the I.S.C. bus, which had pulled up behind them. Students were not allowed to drive their own cars to the I.S.C., except on the first day, when they had to be accompanied by a parent or guardian.

Mr. O'Connor parked the car in front of the building, but no one made a move to get out. Instead, they watched as a straggling bunch of students hurried through the rain and formed an orderly line in front of the entrance doors. Beth was shocked to see a boy, not much older than ten, lined up behind another student who looked as if he should have graduated some years ago. As best she could tell, there was not another girl in the line.

Franklin O'Connor drew in his breath and looked at his family. "Are we ready?" he said. Beth swallowed the rock that had lodged in her throat, and nodded. At the entrance, her father put one hand on the doorknob and the other on Beth's shoulder. He gave her an encouraging smile and said, "This isn't going to be forever, you know."

"That's right," her mother answered. "The district dropped the criminal charges. I'm sure Helen Dycus will release you from here after we talk to her on Monday. We'll get this straightened out. I just know we will."

Beth didn't trust herself to say a word. She had seen the bars on the windows and the familiar claustrophobic feeling from the jail swept over her again. In a gesture that surprised her as much as it did her mother, Beth reached for the older woman's hand and squeezed it. The answering squeeze comforted her, and together the three of them walked into the receiving area of the I.S.C.

The rules and regulations were rigid, and Rosalinda

Costanza, the intake officer, explained them in a monotone to Beth and her parents. Beth would be allowed two rest room breaks a day of three minutes each. She would be accompanied on these breaks by a matron who worked at the center. No excuses were accepted for absences, except court appearances. Ms. Costanza looked at Beth when she came to this part of the document. "Will you be going to court?" she asked.

Force of habit made Beth wait for her mother to answer, and when she didn't, Beth looked in her direction. She could see the muscles constricting in Joanne O'Connor's throat, and her eyes were dangerously wet. Beth had never seen her mother cry before, and she felt her own composure giving way.

"What has that got to do with anything?" Franklin O'Connor's voice showed his anger.

The intake officer went on with her orientation speech. "It has to do with absences," she said coldly. "Many of the students here are awaiting court appearances. If a student is found innocent of whatever he or she is charged with, the absence will be excused. However, if a student is found guilty as charged— even if it is a parking ticket—then the district will not excuse the absence. The student will get zeros for those days he or she appeared in court. Do you understand?" Ms. Costanza let her eyes flick from Beth, to her mother, then to her father.

Joanne O'Connor leaned forward in her seat. "I don't see how you can do that," she said in an even voice. "People are summoned to court. They have no choice about going. Court appearances should be excused absences—regardless of the outcome. Beth and Mr. O'Connor and I have an appointment with Helen Dycus at ten A.M. Monday morning. I expect Beth's absence for that appointment to be excused."

Ms. Costanza acted as if she had heard indignant parents before. "Those are the district's rules," she said impassively, then turned her attention back to her copy of the center's rules and regulations.

"Talking is forbidden, although there may be some conversation at lunch, if it does not get out of hand. Most of our, uh, students are here because they are unable to handle themselves in a normal classroom; that is the purpose of this facility. They are rarely violent, but fights can—and do—happen." She ran her eyes up and down Beth's slight figure. "It would be wise if you remained on the alert at all times. Anyone caught with a weapon, drugs, cigarettes—regular or marijuana—or unsuitable clothing will be immediately expelled. As you can see, we have strict rules, strictly enforced. Is that clear?"

Beth nodded.

"You will be expected to remain seated at your study cubicle, which faces a blank wall. There will be partitions between you and the other students. As I said before, talking is absolutely forbidden, except to address a question to the proctor if you don't understand the lesson plan."

"There isn't a teacher to teach?" Joanne O'Connor's face had turned a deadly white.

"There are prepared lesson plans. The students work on their own."

"But what about the give and take of a classroom?

No one learns by reading a set of lesson plans!" Joanne looked helplessly at her husband, at Beth, and back at Ms. Costanza.

"Most of the students here have very little interest in learning. I'm sure Bethany demonstrated that, or she would not have been sent here."

"That's a lie!" Franklin O'Connor's face was bright red. He slammed his fist on the edge of the woman's desk, making the pencils jump in the orange juice can that held them. "My daughter loves school and has never missed a day of it, unless she was sick. She has no business being here in this . . . this reformatory."

"Your alternative is to allow the district to permanently expel her. Do you want that?" Two pencils had jumped right out of the can, and Beth watched the woman's pudgy fingers shove them back in as she talked. She didn't seem perturbed by Mr. O'Connor's outburst, and Beth supposed she'd seen much worse in the course of a day at the I.S.C.

Ms. Costanza looked at Beth and said, "If you are the kind of student your parents seem to think you are, then I would suggest you bring a few magazines, or perhaps a book, to read. You'll probably get through your lesson plans fast, and you'll need to fill the time. Anything you bring to school—lunches, purse, books, or magazines—must be inspected by me at the beginning of the day. Do you have any questions?"

"I don't have any books," Beth said.

"You'll get them here, but they are not to go home with you."

"What? How's she supposed to study?" Joanne said.

"She'll do her studying here. Our students don't know how to take care of school property," Ms. Costanza said. "Any more questions?"

When no one said anything, the woman rose, like the Angel of Judgment, from her seat behind the desk. "Very well. I'll be taking Beth off to her study cubicle now. The I.S.C. bus will deliver her to your home by approximately four this afternoon."

There was a bulletin board right behind the woman's desk. It displayed a poster with telephone numbers to report child abuse, flyers for various drug rehabilitation programs, and a cartoon that showed a giant male authority figure behind a desk. Underneath the cartoon the caption said, "Right or wrong, I'm always right." Conspicuously missing were announcements of chorale tryouts, tutoring programs by the National Honor Society, football schedules, yearbook sales, upcoming orchestra concerts, or any of the other kinds of flyers that peppered Millington's bulletin boards. Beth swallowed hard and made a great pretense of studying the board while her parents rose and prepared to leave the building.

The door shut slowly after the O'Connors and sealed itself with a heavy click. Ms. Costanza picked up the intake sheets and said, "All right, Bethany. We're ready for you. Come with me."

At lunch a proctor came to get the students and line them up. There was one other girl sentenced to the I.S.C., and a matron took her and Beth—despite Beth's protests that she didn't need to go—to the ladies' rest room. Inside, there were no doors on the stalls; however, the matron sat on a stool in the corner, out of eyesight. Beth studied the other girl carefully as they washed their hands. She guessed her to be thirteen, perhaps fourteen. Her hair was dyed black and shaved close to her head over one ear. Over the other, it hung long. Her jeans were dirty. So, Beth noticed, were her fingernails. "So, what're you in for?" she said to Beth as they wiped their hands on paper towels.

Beth glanced at the matron, wondering if she would be permitted to answer. The matron didn't seem to mind the question, so Beth said, "It's a long story."

"I got time. You could tell me at lunch," the girl said. "I've been here for four weeks. You're the only other girl I've seen. They don't send girls here much."

The matron marched both girls to an empty class-room which served as a lunchroom. There was no cafeteria at the I.S.C. Students were expected to bring a lunch from home. The girl, who said her name was Sabrina, had none. "My mom didn't have time to make it," she said, but Beth noticed her eyes focusing on the turkey, lettuce, and tomato sandwich that she was carefully unwrapping and putting on the napkin in front of her.

"Want half of mine?" Beth said suddenly. "My mom always makes too much." She pushed half the sandwich across the table toward Sabrina, who after only a mo-ment's hesitation laid a proprietary hand on it.

"Keep your voices down," the lunchroom monitor said, then returned to reading her copy of the *National Enquirer*.

"So, what'd you do?" Sabrina asked. Her voice was low, almost conspiratorial.

"It had to do with a football game and a stolen mascot. It's just too complicated to explain. What are you doing here?"

Beth studied Sabrina as they talked. Her clothes were worn and not too clean, and the dyed black hair made her look hard. But her eyes were a pretty color, not green and not brown, shadowed by dark circles.

"I was tardy," Sabrina said sarcastically.

"Late to school? And they sent you here?" Beth was astonished. Tardies at Millington earned students a detention.

"Yeah. Well, they threatened to sue my mom. Get that. What would they sue her for? Our food stamps? Anyway, I'm here."

"I don't understand—" Beth began.

"I didn't expect you to." Sabrina chewed her sandwich hungrily and eyed Beth as if trying to make up her mind about something. Finally she said, "Oh, stuff it. You can't help it if you're rich."

"I'm—we're not rich," Beth said.

"Yeah, and I have a scholarship to Yale," Sabrina retorted. "Do you want me to tell you how I got here, or not?"

"I haven't got anything else to do. Fire away," Beth said as she pushed her trash back into the brown paper sack.

Sabrina began picking at the dirt that was under one fingernail. "If you laugh, you're gonna be sorry, and I mean that. I'll get you."

The ominous tone in Sabrina's voice seemed genuine, and Beth had no trouble at all assuring the girl that she wasn't going to laugh.

Sabrina drew in a deep breath. "Part of my problem was working up the guts to go to school. Every time I thought about going, I got freaked out."

"Well, I get freaked out, too, if I'm not ready for a test or something."

Sabrina gave Beth a disgusted look.

"I'm sorry," Beth said quickly. "Go on."

"I wasn't worried about a stupid test. It was like . . . like snakes or something was waiting for me inside the building. I can't explain it, but believe me, I couldn't go. I'd just as soon have walked into a rattler's nest. As soon as Mom left for work I'd take off and hide out for the day. Drove the district crazy. Half the time, they couldn't find me, and when they did, I'd pitch a fit—kicking, scratching. They never *could* get me to go. At least, not without a fight." The pride in Sabrina's voice was unmistakable.

"You're here now, aren't you?" Beth had decided she really didn't like this girl.

Sabrina ignored Beth's comment. She was intent on finishing her story. "You know why they make us come to school, don't you?"

"Because it's the law," Beth answered.

"Hah! That's what everybody thinks, but it really boils down to money—just like everything else. School districts get paid money every day for each kid who's in school. That's why they have such a fit when we're absent. No kids, no money. That's why they threatened to sue my mom if she didn't get me to school. They didn't want me. They wanted the money."

Beth look at Sabrina skeptically. "Well, all I can say is, I missed two weeks with mono in my sophomore year, and nobody threatened to sue my parents. They sent my work home, and helped me catch up when I got back. Nobody said a word about money."

Sabrina spoke shortly. "Do you want to hear the rest of this story or not?"

"I suppose I don't have a choice," Beth said, looking around the lunchroom. There were a few other conversations going on, but most students were either eating silently or staring sullenly out the window.

"Well, my mom goes off when she thinks we're going to get sued, and she hauls me off to some agency to see a shrink. I'll say this about the doctor, she was pretty cool and she helped me some. Got me to talk some about being afraid. She even got my junior high to send my work home for a while—stuff like that, so I wouldn't get behind. In case you hadn't noticed, I'm not dumb."

Sabrina threw this last comment down as a challenge. "I didn't say you were," Beth snapped back.

"Well, finally my shrink and I decide that I will go back to school on a Monday—okay? Monday comes, my mom goes to work, and I leave for the bus stop. Everything's okay. I get on the bus, get to the school, and suddenly I can't do it. My palms are sweaty and my heart is slamming around in my chest. Everybody else is going in the building, happy as a clam. But the old feelings come over me again. I mean, I am really panicked. I didn't have any money to call my shrink, so I ran. I ran, and I ran, and I ran. When I couldn't run anymore, I sat down and thought. The more I thought, the more determined I got. I'm not a chicken. Nothing scares me, and I wasn't going to let school scare me, either. I went back, and I walked into that building. It was the hardest thing I ever did. I was about an hour and a half late and they counted me absent for the whole day."

"Absent? Why not tardy?" Beth said.

"New rule. Come a half-hour late or more and you're absent for the whole day if you don't have an excuse. They said it was my sixth absence and I automatically had to come here for six weeks."

"But they knew about your problem," Beth protested. "What about your doctor? Didn't she say something to the school officials?"

"That don't make no difference to them," Sabrina said. "They said I was goofing off. Man, they sent a truant officer to the house and said if I didn't show up here on time every day, they'd drag my mom into court. She whaled the tar out of me when he left, and here I am."

"Well, you and your mother should have appealed," Beth said.

"Appealed? Hah! Appeals don't do any good. My mom wouldn't take off work for any appeal." Sabrina looked disgustedly at Beth, who began to fold and unfold her paper napkin.

"What school do you go to? Normally, I mean," Beth asked.

"Rickover Junior High. It's not far from here. I'm in ninth grade."

"When do you go back?" Beth asked.

"My sentence is up in two weeks. I'm supposed to go back then, but I don't know. I've missed a lot of work. It's hard to keep up out here. Nobody wants to help you, you'll see. I asked one of the proctors for some help in algebra, and she said, 'Beats me. I can't teach you this stuff. My degree's in parks and recreation.' " Sabrina laughed out loud. "Can you imagine that? A college degree to run a park? I guess they think this joint's some kind of resort."

"It's too loud over there. Silence till the end of lunch," the monitor said, looking at Beth and Sabrina. At the other three tables, sullen faces stared at the two girls who had caused silence to fall on the lunchroom again.

The rest of the day was wrapped in silence for Beth. She sped through lesson plans that were simple, almost juvenile. Sabrina's story ran round and round in her head. Of course, it might not be true. The girl could be making the entire thing up. Maybe she was here because she stole something, or did drugs. But I'm here, and I didn't steal anything or do any drugs, Beth thought to herself.

In order to fill the time, she rechecked her worksheets—twice. On Monday she'd bring an extra sandwich and some magazines. The ancient clock on the wall made loud ticking sounds. Right above the six, in elaborate but faded lettering, was the motto *Tempus Fugit*. Not in the I.S.C., Beth thought to herself bitterly. She willed herself not to think of Millington and the days that flew by there.

At 3:25 the school bus finally lumbered into the parking lot, its squealing brakes announcing liberation for all. Beth O'Connor's first day at I.S.C. was practically over.

True to Ms. Costanza's word, Beth was dropped off at her home by a few minutes past four. When she came in the front door, her mother immediately terminated her phone conversation and hurried into the den to greet her. "How are you?" she said, peering anxiously at Beth as if she were ill.

"I'm all right," Beth said. "I can take it for a while."

Joanne O'Connor nodded. "Jed called just before you got in. He wanted you to get back to him when you got home."

Beth bolted for the privacy of her bedroom telephone and quickly placed the call. An answering machine came on the line. There was a new message on it that ended, in Adelaide Stuart's chirpy voice, "Go Coogs!" Beth didn't bother to leave a message of her own. She'd try again later.

Beth's mother was emptying the dishwasher when Beth returned to the kitchen. "Did you reach Jed?" she asked.

"He wasn't home. I'll get him later." Beth took a stack of clean plates from her mother and put them in the cupboard.

"I called his father this morning." Joanne O'Connor extracted two butcher knives and slipped them into their rack by the stove.

Beth sank into a kitchen chair. "Why?" she asked warily.

"I told him I wanted to address the school board regarding this district's philosophy of student discipline."

"Mother! You know Mr. Stuart said we needed to cooperate for a while. We haven't even talked to Dr. Dycus yet."

"Well, it doesn't matter. Mr. Stuart informed me I wasn't entitled to a hearing in front of the board. Can you believe it?" Joanne closed the dishwasher and turned to face her daughter. "I don't know, Beth. It looks like our last hope really is Helen Dycus."

"But Mr. Stuart will help me. At least, he will if you don't make any more waves. I promised Jed you wouldn't." Beth was breathing hard and her eyes stung with tears. She hated the I.S.C. With all her heart, she wanted to be back at Millington. She prayed silently that her mother wouldn't ruin her chances. "Remember, Mom, the district dropped the criminal charges."

Beth's mother pulled out a chair and sat at the table, too. "That wasn't an act of charity, Beth. I think they realized that your civil rights had been violated. The entire case would probably have been thrown out of court, anyway." Joanne O'Connor began ticking off points on her fingers. "One. You didn't get read your rights. Two. You weren't permitted a phone call." Mrs. O'Connor slammed her hand down on the kitchen table. "No wonder the district dropped the charges. In a courtroom, they play by the rules, and this district doesn't even obey its own."

"Are you talking about the jurisdiction thing?" Beth asked.

Mrs. O'Connor nodded her head. "That and other things, too. Like not being allowed to address the school board with my grievances. I elect those officials. I have a right to talk to them."

Beth thought of Sabrina saying, "Appeals don't do any good," and felt a small chill go through her. Her mother was still talking as she put place mats on the table.

"Nobody respects anybody's civil rights in this district. If I want to be heard, there's only one place to go. Court."

"Mother! Don't jump to conclusions—that's what you always tell me," Beth said. "We don't know what Dr. Dycus will say."

Joanne O'Connor sighed. "You could be right," she said, then glanced at the clock on the kitchen wall. "Look at the time! Run down to the stables and get Ruthie for me, okay? She's been working with Dunney long enough, and I want an early dinner tonight."

"I'll ride my bike," Beth said, glad to leave the house and the conversation behind. She wheeled her ancient Schwinn out of the garage, kicked up the stand, and took off for the stables in search of her sister.

CHAPTER

ELEVEN

The stables sounded much more elegant than they were. They consisted of crudely constructed barns, riding trails, and a corral. Beth found Ruthanne in the corral practicing her barrel racing. She was working Dunney on the turns, coaxing the quarterhorse to take them as close to the barrels as possible. When Ruthanne saw Beth, she called out to her, "Time me on this run. I've got to shave some seconds off, or I'll never win."

Beth parked the bike against the corral's fence, and leaned against it to watch her sister ride. Ruthanne gave Dunney a kick, and the two of them were off, racing around the three orange barrels in a cloverleaf pattern. When she was finished, Ruthanne galloped up

137

to the fence. "How long did it take?" she asked, panting for breath.

"Less than a minute. Maybe thirty seconds. I can't really tell with a watch like this," Beth said, looking at the small face on her wristwatch.

"That's not good enough," Ruthanne said. "I have to come in at twenty seconds or under. Those girls from Simonton fly."

"When's the competition?" Beth asked.

"In about a month. If I get to do it."

"What do you mean, 'if I get to do it'? You always compete. One of these days you're going to win a buckle or whatever it is that barrel racers win."

"It's a buckle," Ruthanne affirmed. "But you can't compete without paying entry fees, and I don't know if Dad'll have the money now that we're going to file your dumb lawsuit."

Beth was incredulous. How could Ruthanne know anything about a lawsuit? As far as Beth was concerned it was merely an idea her mother was considering. She looked at her sister and said, "Don't worry. Nobody's filing any lawsuits."

Ruthanne slipped out of the saddle and looped Dunney's reins over a post. "Well, all I know is Mom's hot about not getting to address the school board. She was telling Dad all about it on the telephone when I came home from school. She's also mad because somebody told her John Bartlett's probably going to play football Saturday night."

"You know Mother. She just likes to blow off steam. I talked to her right before I came over here, and I calmed her down. Everything will be all right after we have our meeting with Dr. Dycus. I'm sure of it."

Ruthanne looked at her sister and nodded. "What's it like?" she said. "The I.S.C."

"It's awful—I don't want to talk about it." Beth shuddered and shook her head, then brightened. "But I'll be out soon, and this'll all be behind us. So don't worry. No lawyer is going to get your entry fee money."

Ruthanne looked at her sister, digesting what she had said. "Maybe you're right." She began to rub Dunney on his nose. "I really want to time him right now, and I didn't bring my stopwatch. You wouldn't want to run home and get it, would you?" she asked.

"No, I wouldn't," Beth answered firmly. "It's getting late, and I'm getting cold. Mom wants an early dinner, so we ought to go now."

Ruthanne looked disappointed, then her face brightened. "Tiffany Stuart has a stopwatch. I've seen it in her tack room. Let's go see if she's here." Ruthanne slipped under the split-rail fence and headed over to the section of the stables that held the tack rooms and barns for the horses.

Beth followed, wondering if she might run into Jed. Sometimes he came to pick up Tiffany, and Beth had always enjoyed these chance encounters with him. They used to walk along the bayou and talk while their sisters exercised their horses.

Ruthanne's voice interrupted Beth's thoughts. "Rats. Nobody's here."

The area around the Stuarts' stall was empty. No

familiar Bronco, no bike leaned against a fence. The only occupant was Tiffany Stuart's horse, who looked up at the approach of the two girls. Ruthanne spoke to him in a familiar, soothing tone. "How ya doing, Fresco, old boy?" The horse looked at the girls with momentary interest, snorted, then went back to munching his dinner of sweet oats.

"I really wanted to time Dunney while he's so warmed up," Ruthanne said. "I think I'll just borrow the watch, anyway."

"The tack room's locked, Ruthie," Beth said, tilting her head toward a combination lock that hung from the battered wooden door.

"No problem," her sister said cheerfully. "I know the combination. Tiffany had me open it once for her, and I remembered it. It's twelve-three-four. Get it? One, two, three, four. Clever, huh?" Ruthanne went over to the lock and began twisting its dial. Within a minute, the loop separated from the round cylinder. Ruthanne tugged on the stubborn door until its rusty hinges let it swing open enough for her to disappear inside. When she didn't emerge with the stopwatch right away, Beth called to her.

"If it's not sitting out on something, Ruthanne, forget it. Tiffany probably took it home with her. Hurry up. We really need to go."

Ruthanne emerged from the tack room, empty-handed and white-faced.

"What's the matter with you?" Beth asked. "You look like you've seen a ghost."

"I may have," her sister answered.

"What? What is it?" Beth said, trying to peer over her sister's shoulder into the gloomy darkness of the simple room.

"Have a look, but you'd better not get your finger-prints on anything. You're in enough trouble as it is."

Beth walked slowly into the tack room. The first thing that struck her was the smell. It was a distinctive, earthy one—a mixture of oats, and hay, and ointments. Horse blankets, bridles, saddles, shovels—all the par-aphernalia of horsemanship—were tossed around the narrow room, helter-skelter. Dust motes danced in a crack of waning sunlight that came through the open door. Beth had trouble adjusting her eyes to the mixture of sunlight and shadow for a minute, and she squinted as she looked for whatever it was that had upset Ruthanne. When she saw it, her heart lurched in her chest. She thought she might throw up, and she fought the impulse to run, run, run—all the way to Galveston, if necessary.

In the corner, awkwardly covered by blankets that had partially fallen away, stood Millington's Crouch-ing Cougar, in perfect condition.

❧ *CHAPTER* ❧

T W E L V E

"What are you going to do?" Ruthanne's freckles stood out on her white face, reminding Beth of the time her sister had been so sick with chicken pox. Both girls were waiting for the light to change at Washington Drive, so they could wheel their bikes across the boulevard.

"I don't know, Ruthie. I've got to talk to Jed before I do or say anything, so that means keeping our mouths shut in front of Mom and Dad, do you understand?"

"They're gonna find out, you know that," Ruthanne said matter-of-factly, before she pushed the bike across the street.

"Maybe not," Beth said, catching up with her on the

other side. Both girls swung themselves onto the seats and pedaled toward home. Beth looked at Ruthanne. "There's an explanation for this. There has to be. I don't want to say anything until I understand what's going on. You have to promise me, not a word. Not right now."

When they reached home, Ruthanne burst through the back door calling, "We're home, and I'm starving."

"Your father's not home yet, so hang on," Joanne said. "Both of you smell like horses and dirt. Go wash up."

Ruthanne and Beth exchanged looks and headed toward the bathroom they both used. Beth turned on the water and used its noise to cover her voice. "I've got to call Jed now. Before we go to dinner. Stay with me . . . in my room, okay? You can head Mother off if she tries to come in."

Ruthanne looked at Beth closely. She could see her sister's hands shaking, so she nodded solemnly. "If you want, I could keep Mom in the den, talking about Dunney or something," she offered.

"No, I need you with me. I don't want to talk to Jed by myself. He's already called once this afternoon, but I wasn't here. Maybe he wanted to explain about the cougar. Maybe he or Carl or somebody just found the cougar and they put it there until tomorrow, till they could return it to school or show it off at the game."

Ruthanne shook her head. "I don't think so. There was dust all over its head. It's been sitting there for a while."

Beth turned the water off and the two girls filed out

of the bathroom and into Beth's bedroom. Ruthanne flopped on the bed and watched Beth as she picked up the receiver and punched in Jed's telephone number. Adelaide Stuart answered the phone. Beth wondered if it was her imagination, or was there a new coolness in the woman's voice? She drew in her breath and was surprised that it entered her lungs in jerky little gasps as she waited for Jed to come to the phone.

"Hey, Babe. What's up?" Jed's voice was normal, even casual, as if this were an evening like any other.

"Not much. I'm . . . I'm just returning your call. Mom said you called earlier."

"Oh, that. Yeah. Well." Beth could hear Jed clear his throat. He was uncomfortable—Beth could tell—and she tried to help him out by providing an encouraging "Yes?" on her end of the line.

The words came out in a rush, as if he wanted to get the bad taste of them out of his mouth. "John's going to get to play tomorrow."

"You said that might happen," Beth answered. Her fingers were weaving through the loops in the telephone cord as if she were playing an instrument. Finally, she drew in a shaky breath. "What about me, Jed? How long am I going to be at the I.S.C.? Has your father said anything else about helping me?"

"Well, uh, that's why I called. My dad saw the police report. They have it down at the administration building. It says you had paint on your hands. John and Carl didn't, you know? Their hands were clean, so to speak." Jed made a feeble attempt at laughter, but Beth ignored it. "Anyway, Dad said it's going to be hard to help you, since it's real obvious that you painted up some stuff."

The muscles in Beth's neck tightened like a vise, and she knew from experience that a severe headache was on its way. In a dull voice she said, "I see. I guess it also looks like I cut the tennis nets and ripped up the gym mats."

"Everybody knows you didn't do all that stuff, Beth," Jed said. "And anyway, they've already dropped the criminal charges, haven't they? I'm just calling because I'm your friend and I want you to know what's going on. I don't want you to get mad at me. You're not, are you? It's not my fault."

Beth pictured Jed sitting on the edge of his bed, his blue eyes troubled, maybe running his hand through his dark hair. The feelings that had swept over her when she and Martha decorated his bedroom swept over her again, and she swallowed hard. "I'm not mad, Jed, but I'm confused," she said, glancing at Ruthanne, who had moved from the bed and was sitting cross-legged on the floor, alternately trying to hear what Beth was saying and keeping an ear out for a parent's footstep in the hall. Beth reached out for her sister's hand and held it as she asked the next question. "There's just one more thing I need to know."

"Fire away," Jed said confidently.

"Ruthanne and I were at the stables this afternoon; she was working out on Dunney. She needed to borrow Tiffany's stopwatch, so she let herself into your tack room. What's the cougar doing in there, Jed?"

Beth felt a sharp pain as her class ring bit into her finger. Ruthanne, her bottom lip caught between her teeth, was squeezing her hand hard, and Beth could feel her own heart thumping and pounding in her temples. The silence on the other end of the phone was thick, like someone had stuffed the telephone lines with cotton. Finally, Jed spoke.

"The tack room was locked," he began.

"Ruthanne knew the combination—Tiffany told it to her. How long has the cougar been there?" Beth asked this question, praying the answer would shed some light on this entire mess, but instead Jed said, "I'm not sure."

"Not sure? Didn't you put it there? Maybe you were at Woodrow Monday night, Jed, who knows? Warning or not, at least some football players were over there. I know. I saw them. But it doesn't matter who found it over there, you're the one who's got it now. Why are you hiding it? Why didn't you bring it back to school?"

"Listen, Beth, it's a complicated story. I . . . I can't explain it now."

"You'd better try, Jed, or else . . . or else I may have to find out on my own. I have a right to know." Beth's voice was calm now, full of resolution.

Jed drew in his breath. "All right. I'll tell you; then maybe you'll feel better about things, but you have to keep it to yourself. Promise?"

"I don't know," Beth answered. "I'm tired of promising things."

"Oh, Beth." Jed's voice sounded miserable. "All right. My father put it there."

Beth felt light-headed, woozy, and for a moment she wondered if perhaps she was going to faint. A vision of Alice, falling through the tunnel into Wonderland, flashed in her head. She was in Wonderland. Nothing made any sense at all. "Your father?" she repeated stupidly.

"Yeah. He said he's worried about the vandalism in the district, you know, and he felt it was getting out of hand, so he put the mascot in Tiffany's tack room so Woodrow kids wouldn't break in and steal it."

"But that doesn't make any sense. I mean, Mr. Pugh and your father and everybody else—including you— let all of us think it was stolen. Y'all knew we wanted revenge. Somebody should have told us it was okay. Somebody should have stopped us." Her mind raced back to the sagging tennis nets and the paint on the buff-colored bricks of Woodrow. She thought of the crates of peppers and tomatoes, the ghostly figures hanging from the trees in the park. All because of a stolen mascot that wasn't stolen at all.

"It sure boosted school spirit," Jed said lamely. "Even your sister got excited."

When Beth finally spoke her voice betrayed all of the misery that she felt. "I've got to go. I'll talk to you later," she said, and replaced the phone on the hook.

When Beth and Ruthanne walked into the kitchen, they saw that their father had arrived home and was finishing a conversation with their mother, who was mashing potatoes at the stove.

Ruthanne looked hard at Beth, nodded her head encouragingly, and mouthed, "Go ahead." The adrenaline poured through Beth's blood. Once this cat was out of the bag, she knew it would be impossible to get it back in. She drew in a breath. "They've found the cougar," she said.

The mashing suddenly stopped. "Oh they did, did they?" her mother said. "Well, where in the world did Woodrow have it?"

"I found it," Ruthanne said, hardly able to contain herself. "It never was at Woodrow. I found it in Tiffany Stuart's tack room. It was all covered up with blankets, but it's okay. It's just fine."

"Slow down," Franklin O'Connor said. "Are you saying it's been in the Stuarts' tack room all this time?"

Beth nodded her head. "I don't know exactly how or when it got there, but the Stuarts knew about it. Jed knew about it, too. He had to."

Joanne O'Connor gave the potatoes another vicious jab and scooped them into a bowl. "I'm sorry. I can't tolerate this. It's utterly ridiculous. What in the world could have motivated the Stuarts to do a thing like that?"

"Jed says his father was worried about vandalism," Beth said.

"I don't believe that for a minute," Franklin O'Connor said. "I think that fool just wanted to heighten the rivalry between the schools. And he had to have help. I'm sure Pugh was in on it, too."

Beth and Ruthanne looked at each other in shock.

"Not necessarily," their mother said. "Since he's president of the school board, I'm sure Jed Stuart had access to Millington without Pugh's help. But it doesn't matter. Pugh may know about it now, and if he does, he's protecting Stuart. It's obvious to me that the adults are in some kind of collusion—no wonder they dropped the criminal charges! They were hoping this entire mess would go away." Joanne O'Connor jabbed her fork into a piece of meat. "I don't think I can let them get away with this. I definitely think we should file a lawsuit. I was going to bring this up even if the girls hadn't found the cougar."

"On what grounds, Jo?" Franklin O'Connor looked weary. "I thought we were through with talk of lawyers and courts."

"Violation of a student's civil rights, that's grounds enough. They do have them, you know—despite what this school district seems to think. Beth didn't even have a hearing—Pugh announced her punishment over the P.A. system before she was even out of jail. And a school simply can't have a policy that gives it the right to punish students for behavior that takes place on their own time. That's the job of the parents—or the police if a person breaks the law." Joanne looked at each member of her family. "Do you all understand what I'm saying?" she asked.

"Trudy Hall went to St. Agnes Academy all last year when her parents were in Saudi Arabia," said Ruthanne, "and she told me that the school could do anything it wanted to. If those girls were bad on Saturday, they got their movie passes taken away on Saturday night. I don't see where that's much different from what's happening to Beth."

"St. Agnes is a private school, honey," said Franklin O'Connor. "It's different with private schools because people choose to go to them. And the school really was taking the place of Trudy's parents, since they were in Saudi Arabia. But Millington wasn't taking our place last Monday night. That's what your mother is trying to say." Franklin O'Connor looked at his daughter. "You need to understand that it's going to be hard on all of us if we decide to go through with a lawsuit."

Beth took a sip of her iced tea. "Lawsuits cost money, and I thought we were worrying about money," she said.

"Am I the only one who's angry around here?" Joanne O'Connor demanded. "You really surprise me, Beth. I thought you had more spunk. Here you are at the I.S.C., losing your education for the next six weeks, and John Bartlett's going to play ball tomorrow night as if nothing had happened."

"He was suspended for a while," Beth said lamely.

Mrs. O'Connor shook her head. "Honey, try to see what I'm saying. The principle here is much bigger than football or suspension or even the I.S.C. The issue is how this school district is run, from the administration to the school board itself." Beth opened her mouth to say something and Joanne interrupted. "I know what you're thinking. That Dr. Dycus will let you out of the I.S.C. It's possible that she will, but that won't change anything about Jed Stuart's or Willard Pugh's behavior. For them, everything takes a backseat to football. If someone doesn't try to clean up this system, more and more students are going to suffer."

"Why do we have to be the ones to do it?" Beth's eyes filled with tears at the thought of a lawsuit.

"Because it doesn't look like anyone else is willing," her mother answered.

"I want to ride Dunney at Simonton," Ruthanne said stubbornly.

"You'll ride the horse. Somehow we'll manage that," her father said.

"Do I have to tell you right now?" Beth asked.

"Take some time to think about it," her father answered. "I'm sick of this depressing subject. Who wants dessert?"

"Me," said Ruthanne. "I want ice cream—vanilla with Hershey's syrup and pecans."

Ruthanne and Beth fixed dessert for everyone, then cleaned up the kitchen. When they were finished Beth tossed a damp washcloth at Ruthanne and said, "Wipe off the table, will you? Barney wants to go for his walk. I'll take him."

The dog was frantically scratching at the back door, and Beth leaned over to snap his red leash onto his collar. She needed a chance to absorb everything that had happened this day, and she wanted to do it alone, away from the house.

There was a harvest moon in the sky, and it lit Beth's street with an almost artificial intensity. Barney tugged on his leash, pulling Beth down the tree-shaded road toward the small elementary school that she and Ruthanne had attended. A creek ran through the back part of the school property, and the dog loved to wade in its shallow, muddy waters.

As Beth and Barney passed the darkened school, she yielded to an impulse and went over to look in her first-grade classroom. She had forgotten for the moment that she was not to set foot on school district property while she was on suspension or attending the I.S.C. The classroom was decorated for Halloween. Ghosts and pumpkins and witches covered the bulletin boards. Beth smiled in spite of herself. The reading circle looked just as it had when Beth was there eleven years ago—eight chairs in a circle by the bookcases in the corner of the room. What was the name of her reading group? She remembered that it was the top one, a distinction that she took quite seriously even then. The Tigers. That was it. That's what they were called.

School had been such fun then. She loved Mrs. Knorr with all her heart, almost as much as she did her mother. Voices from the past filled her head. "*W*," they said. "*W* sounds like *wishbone*." Mrs. Knorr would hold up a picture of a giant wishbone, and everyone in the group would repeat, "Wuhh. Wishbone." Once, Beth had taken a wishbone to school, and she and Mrs. Knorr had wished on it together and broken it. Beth had gotten the bigger half, and her teacher hugged her. "Don't tell your wish, or it won't come true," she'd said. How could the little girl sitting in that circle so long ago have wound up where she was today?

CHAPTER

THIRTEEN

The day of the big game passed far more pleasantly for Beth than she had imagined it would, probably because she didn't spend it in Fort Preston. Instead, her father borrowed a cabin on Lake Titusville from one of his customers at the bank, and insisted that the entire family spend the day there "away from radios, televisions, football, and Fort Preston." Everyone, including Ruthanne, had agreed that it was a good idea. Ruthanne and her father had gone fishing, while Beth and her mother walked in the woods. No one talked about the events of the preceding week or about the possibility of a lawsuit. It was as if there was a conspiracy of silence among all the O'Connors. This Saturday was theirs, and they hung on to it, not leaving the lake to return to Fort Preston until nearly midnight.

The feeling of well-being held through Sunday morning as the entire family dressed for church. Although her parents often questioned the "give in order to get" theology that laced the sermons of their preacher, Brother Billy John Offet, the O'Connors, like most of their friends, were in attendance at the First Community Church more Sundays than they were not.

The church was large—the biggest in Fort Preston—and its parking lot was almost full when the O'Connors arrived. They were running late and Beth, for once, was glad. She didn't want to see anyone. Jed's father was a deacon, and the entire Stuart family often lingered in the vestibule of the church greeting visitors and members alike, as if they were welcoming them into their own home. Under normal circumstances Beth enjoyed these chances to visit with Jed while the adults swapped pleasantries. It amused her to watch her father, eager to end the conversation and get seated, try to cut the talk short. But there would be no pleasantries this morning if her parents saw the Stuarts. Beth knew that her parents would demand an accounting from Mr. Stuart for the cougar's disappearance, and she didn't want that to happen here. She was glad to see that the choir had already assembled. That meant the Stuarts would have already taken their place in the second pew on the right, a pew that everyone tacitly understood was reserved for them.

The organist was playing something soothing as a

154

prelude, and Beth and her parents quietly slipped into a pew near the back. Several rows ahead, she caught a glimpse of Martha, sitting with several other Millington seniors. On a normal Sunday Beth might have joined them. For today, she was glad she was with her family.

The organist segued from the prelude into a rousing chorus of "All Hail the Power of Jesus' Name," and Brother Billy John, brandishing his Bible and flanked by his two assistants, emerged from behind the altar. He raised his arms as the maroon-robed choir poured down the aisles, urging the congregation to its feet to join in the singing of the hymn.

". . . crown him Lord of all." The last words of the hymn faded and everyone settled back into the pews. Brother Billy John stood behind the lectern and made the usual assortment of announcements about the Bible studies, the evening service, the needs of the missionaries, the state of the budget, and the upcoming meeting of the Ladies' Society. Then he shook his great white mane of hair, and let his piercing blue eyes scan his flock slowly. "I know our hearts are heavy this morning, sisters and brothers, and I just wonder if you'll pray with me?"

Without waiting for an answer, Brother Billy John took his worn Bible and laid it in front of the altar, then promptly knelt upon it. Beth had seen him do this before, but only when things were getting pretty serious, like the time a Bible study group in the church began to question whether every story in the Bible was literally true.

"O God," began the Reverend, "our hearts are heavy within us this morning. What we had so hoped would be a glorious accounting of our young men on the football field has turned into something less. Our warriors have fallen."

"Millington must have lost," Ruthanne whispered to Beth, who then poked her sister in the ribs to silence her.

"Indeed, one of our own is wounded and we don't know if he will ever play the game again."

Beth's eyes sprang open and she searched the Stuarts' pew. There were people in it, but not Jed's family. Goose bumps popped out on her flesh, and she saw Martha take the back of her hand to the corner of her eye.

"I am calling upon you to restore a clean heart in us all. Cleanse us of vengeance and keep us from feeling ill will toward our brothers, whether we win or whether we lose. We ask this and put it under the blood of Jesus. A-men."

Brother Billy John heaved himself up, and one of his assistants retrieved the Bible. The elderly minister then resumed his place behind the lectern. "Now I have a word for you young people," he said, his eyes under the bushy white eyebrows scanning his flock and coming to rest upon a hapless teenager who sat in the third row. "Football is a wonderful, wonderful game and it has produced some of this state's finest citizens, including one of our very own deacons, a man who tithes his full tenth to the work of the Lord." At this point Brother Billy John looked significantly toward the Stuarts' pew. "But trouble has come upon us, and upon the Stuart family, and it happened in the name of football. Last night's game got out of hand, and I think we all know why. Tempers flared. Unchristian-like conduct took place. I want all the young people of Fort Preston to examine their hearts and ask forgiveness for what they have done and offer forgiveness to those who have hurt them. Now, we will proceed with the offertory, while Sister Thelma Johnstone sings 'The Spacious Firmament on High.' "

The rest of the service was agony for Beth. During the sermon she and Ruthanne scribbled notes to each other on the blank backs of the pledge cards, and for once, neither of their parents tried to stop them.

"What do you think happened?" Ruthanne wrote. "What'd he mean, 'We all know why'? Does he mean the trouble with you?"

"I dunno," Beth wrote back. "I'll try to catch Martha as soon as we get out."

"Do you think Jed's going to die?" Ruthanne wrote. Beth looked at her sister carefully. She was truly frightened.

"It can't be that bad. He said something about not playing football again. Just pray, Ruthie, pray." This time Beth didn't write it, but whispered into Ruthanne's ear.

The service ended with a rousing rendition of "I Love to Tell the Story." Beth thought she would explode if the choir didn't hurry up and leave. She persuaded her parents to avoid shaking hands with Brother Offet and to leave by a side door. "I need to talk to Martha," she explained, and was grateful when neither parent questioned her further.

In the parking lot she saw Martha hurrying toward the station wagon. Beth called, "Martha, wait up," and the girl looked over her shoulder and slowed down.

"What's happened?" Beth said when she finally was face to face with her friend.

"I can't believe you don't know," Martha answered. "Jed's been hurt. Bad. It was all over the radio. Didn't you listen to the game?"

Beth looked at Martha. "I wasn't here" was all she said. She knew that any further explanation would be wasted on Martha. The retreat to Lake Titusville would be another act of a world-class wuss. "Just tell me what happened."

"Jed got sacked from behind on practically every play during the third quarter. It was awful. There were Woodrow kids all over him—they were practically insane, they were so mad. It must have been the way he fell, or maybe it was the fact that he fell so often, but Jed broke his leg. There were red flags all over the field—penalties for unnecessary roughness. Then a fistfight broke out, before they could even carry him off the field. A lot of guys got hurt, but Jed got the worst of it."

Beth was astonished. She'd never seen that kind of violence at a football game. "What got Woodrow that riled up? We're the ones who should have been mad."

"You haven't heard about the eagle, huh?" Despite the seriousness of the conversation, Beth could tell that

Martha was delighted to be the first one to fill her in. "It got stolen from Woodrow."

"Who took it?" Beth interrupted.

"It was the work of a committee, but Carl was its chairman."

"Oh, no!" Beth groaned, remembering her conversation with Carl on Thursday. This must have been what he was talking about when he said the cougar had been avenged.

"Oh, yes, and it gets worse. You know how that eagle is painted mostly yellow, with a red collar?"

Beth nodded, urging Martha to get on with it.

"Well, they sprayed it green and black all over, then Carl took a shotgun and blew holes all through its chest and knocked off its tailfeathers. It looked like a bedraggled parrot when the guys were finished with it."

"What was the point of all this?" Beth asked.

"Well, they had our mascot, didn't they? At least that's what all of us thought, but then, lo and behold, our beloved Crouching Cougar shows up right before the game in our locker room, safe and sound. I can tell you, Carl and I were never so happy to see anything in our whole lives. The bad thing is, some of the kids thought it would be real funny to roll the cougar out at halftime, then drag this wounded bird out onto the field right behind it. It turned out not to be such a good idea. That's when the playing got dirty and Jed got hurt."

"What's happened to Carl?" Beth could picture him, his face flushed with anger, spraying paint at Woodrow's plaster eagle. But shooting it was another matter. The thought made her feel sick.

"He got into the free-for-all on the football field after Jed got hurt. Coach pulled him off by his tail. You should have seen it; it would have been funny if it hadn't been so bad. Somebody ratted and told that Carl was the one who shot the bird. He's been expelled from school."

"Where is he now?" Beth asked.

"I don't know. Home, I guess. Jed's at Mercy Hospital. They operated late last night. Listen, I've gotta go. Mother wants the car this afternoon." She fished in her purse for the keys. When she pulled her hand out, she also had an envelope in it. It was filled with one-, five-, and ten-dollar bills, plus some change. Martha offered the envelope to Beth, saying "Take it, it's yours. There's about two hundred and fifty dollars there, believe it or not. I counted it last night."

"Where'd you get it?" Beth asked.

"From everybody. I used a little extortion when I had to, but there's no point in you having to pay for the damage at Woodrow all by yourself."

"We can't even get Mr. Pugh to tell us exactly what we owe."

"Well, I'm sure this won't cover everything, but it's the best I could do," Martha said. She unlocked the car door, then looked at Beth again. "Listen. If you find out that you're going to need more money, come back to me. I'll organize a car wash or something. That's it. The Beth O'Connor Car Wash. It might even be fun."

Beth swallowed hard and felt tears sting her eyes. "Thanks, Martha," was all she managed to say.

"What are friends for?" the girl answered cheerily. Then she added, "I gotta go, but I'll call you tomorrow. I want to hear all about the I.S.C."

Beth nodded and turned to join her family, who were waiting by their car in the now-deserted parking lot. On the way home, Beth filled them in on what Martha had told her. Franklin O'Connor's hands tightened around the steering wheel as she talked, and she noticed a red flush creeping up the back of his neck.

"This has got to stop," he said. "This . . . this mania . . . is out of hand. I'd like to subpoena Jed Sr., and Willard Pugh and maybe even Helen Dycus—the whole lot of them. I'd like to put them on the stand and get them to tell all of Fort Preston what they know. First, they steal their own mascot just to whip the student body up, then the duped Millington kids go over to Woodrow to try to get it back. When they can't find it, they steal Woodrow's eagle in retaliation."

"And promptly trash it up," Joanne O'Connor added disgustedly.

"And kids wind up without education, teeth, or legs." Franklin O'Connor caught Beth's eye in his rearview mirror. "Honey, this district doesn't care about education. At least, not as much as it does about winning football games. Willard Pugh doesn't have the courage to back away from a bad decision. It takes a big man to admit when he's wrong, and Pugh is small. The trouble is, he's also in charge of hundreds of kids' education. He's in thick with the school board, and I imagine Helen Dycus will back him up tomorrow. Nothing's going to change without a lawsuit. Have you thought any more about it?"

"All I know is I want to go to the hospital to see Jed," Beth answered. They were home by now, and Beth had already kicked off her high heels and was busily soothing the hysterically excited Barney by rubbing him behind his ears.

"Want your mother or me to go with you?" her father said.

Beth shook her head. "Thanks, Dad, but no. I want to go by myself. I really do. I just want to see how he feels, tell him how I feel. I've got to go alone."

Joanne O'Connor sighed. She handed Beth the keys to her car, then as an afterthought added, "Don't forget to fasten your seatbelt."

C H A P T E R

F O U R T E E N

Beth hated hospitals. The squeaky sound of the nurses'
rubber-soled shoes on the shiny floors, the half-closed
doors, the knots of people standing around talking in
whispers, a few jovial doctors swapping jokes and
laughing—all frightened her. A disembodied voice
came over the loudspeaker. "Dr. Gerlich. Dr. Gerlich.
You're needed in emergency. Stat."

Orthopedics was on the third floor, and Beth stood
before the bank of elevators, punching "3" more than
was necessary. After an eternity, the car arrived and
swept her upward. At the third floor, the elevator
doors slid open silently, and she faced a busy nurses'
station. A nurse's aide indicated that Jed was in room
307, and tossed her head to the left as she said it. "He's

had a stream of visitors all afternoon, but we're only letting them in for a few minutes. Everybody's in the waiting room down there." The woman pointed to a sign that had an arrow and "Rooms 300–315" painted on it, and Beth obediently turned in that direction.

The waiting room was full. Jed's parents were there, receiving kids as if they were hosting a reception. Beth noticed that John Bartlett had his arm in a cast. ". . . just a broken wrist," she heard him tell someone.

Jed Sr., flanked by his wife, was talking to Mr. Pugh. "A little therapy . . . hell, a lot of therapy, and we'll have that leg ready for U.T., you'll see. Nothing stops my boy."

Adelaide Stuart's eyes met Beth's and she smiled slightly. "Why, Bethany, what a surprise," she said.

"Well, now. Hello, Bethany," Willard Pugh said. He was chewing on a cigar that remained unlit in his mouth.

Beth managed a nod at Mr. Pugh. It would have to pass for hello. Mr. Pugh began to talk to Mr. Stuart. Mr. Stuart nodded his head seriously and put a hand on Mr. Pugh's elbow, guiding him into an isolated corner of the waiting room to finish the conversation.

Beth turned her attention to Adelaide Stuart. "I heard what happened to Jed. Just this morning, in church. Brother Billy John talked about it." Beth felt as if she were using her second-year Spanish, spitting out short sentences as if the language was new to her.

"Well, how lovely of him," Adelaide said.

"I, uh, well, I had sort of hoped I could see Jed,"

Beth said. "I just wanted to tell him how sorry I am about . . . about everything."

Adelaide Stuart led Beth down the hall. Quietly, she pushed open the door to Jed's room. "Don't stay long," she said and disappeared.

Beth stepped into the room and glanced quickly at the bed. Jed, almost the color of his sheets, opened his eyes and gave her a weak smile. He wiggled his fingers in a kind of wave, but Beth noticed that he didn't even lift his hand from the coverlet where it lay. His left leg was encased in plaster and hoisted up at an unnatural angle. She managed a weak smile and said, "Jed, I'm so sorry. Does it hurt awfully bad?" Beth glanced at his leg, then at the intravenous tubes that fed into both arms and snaked out from under his covers.

"Doesn't feel good," he said. "But I'm due another pain shot soon."

Beth was shocked at the hoarseness in his voice—it was more of a croak that cut off suddenly, as the pain gripped again. "Want me to call for the nurse?" Beth asked as a kind of panic gripped her. She had never seen anyone hurt this much.

Jed shook his head. Beads of perspiration dotted his upper lip. "Dad . . . says to . . . tough it out . . . as long as I can." He let out a sigh. The effort of speaking had exhausted him.

"I'll go tell your dad it's time, Jed." Beth walked over to the bed and gingerly touched his arm. "I'll come back later. When you're feeling better, okay?"

Jed tried to smile, but it came out more like a grimace, and Beth hurried from the room to tell Jed's parents that he needed his shot. Now. Adelaide hurried off in the direction of the nurses' station, leaving Beth face to face with Mr. Stuart.

"Mother and Dad said to tell you they hope Jed gets better quickly," Beth began, "and I'm sorry . . . sorry things got out of hand," she said, wishing she were more articulate.

Jed Stuart drew in his breath and let it go with a loud whoosh. "I'd say 'out of hand' is a real understatement, young lady. It was nothing short of a massacre on that field Saturday night. We're real lucky Jed wasn't killed."

"I'm glad I didn't see it," Beth said truthfully.

"It wasn't pretty, believe you me. And to top it off, we lost. So that's that, I guess. No championship for the Millington Cougars. It's just too bad."

Beth stared at Mr. Stuart in astonishment, then drew in her breath. "Mr. Stuart, I really need to talk to you. Can we find a place to sit down . . . away from everybody?"

Jed Stuart looked around the waiting room. Mr. Pugh had left and only a few football players remained. They were talking among themselves by the soda machine. Beth thought Mr. Stuart looked irritated, but nevertheless, he led her to two empty seats in the far corner. "What's on your mind, missy?" he said.

"The I.S.C., sir," Beth said in a rush. "Jed said that I might not have to go . . . at least, not for long, and I was . . . well, I was hoping you could do something about it."

"Wait a minute," Jed Stuart said, leaning forward and peering straight at Beth. "My son's in there with a broken leg and a possibly ruined football career, and you're asking me to worry about a few paltry weeks in the I.S.C.? You're lucky you didn't get expelled, right along with that Loessing kid."

Beth reeled back as if she had taken a physical blow. "But John Bartlett got to play Saturday night," she began.

". . . And ask him if he's happy about it. Now he's got a broken arm. Thanks to you crazy kids."

"But you're the one who took the cougar and hid it in the first place! If you hadn't done that, Jed wouldn't be here right now." Beth had no intentions of uttering this statement. It just popped out as if it had a will of its own. There was a moment of shocked silence in which Beth suddenly realized that Jed had not told his father that she and Ruthanne had discovered the cougar. Mr. Stuart was a good politician, however, and he quickly recovered his composure. "I wouldn't be so quick to jump to conclusions, young lady. And I might add that you had no business breaking into my family's tack room. It's always locked."

"I know that," Beth whispered. "Ruthanne just wanted to borrow Tiffany's stopwatch."

Mr. Stuart smiled encouragingly. "Well now, I understand. And that makes my point. Sometimes things aren't what they appear to be. It appeared that you two young ladies were breaking and entering, but in reality, you were just borrowing the stopwatch. Sometimes people make choices that aren't the best. Hell, sometimes we've got to choose between bad and worse, don't we?"

"Mr. Stuart, what about the school's choices? Mr.

Pugh said I was guilty before I ever got out of jail. He even had my suspension notice filled out! And the school board's own rules say that I was on my own time when I . . . when I painted the car."

"So by your own admission you did some damage."

"I wish, I wish I'd never told the truth!" Tears welled in Beth's eyes. It was true—she should have kept her mouth shut.

"It's always best to tell the truth, Bethany," Mr. Stuart said sanctimoniously.

"Mother says you won't even let her come to the school board and talk about what happened. Now my folks are talking about a lawsuit and I . . . I don't want one, but I can't blame them. I . . . we just don't understand what's going on. Are you going to tell other kids the truth about taking the cougar?"

Mr. Stuart frowned. "A lawsuit. Of all the crazy . . . you won't win, I can tell you that." He made a pretense of looking at the clock on the wall. "I see no point in continuing this conversation." Suddenly his mood shifted again from the quick anger of a moment ago to conciliation. He draped an arm across Beth's shoulders and propelled her toward the elevator banks. "I need to see if Jed's gotten his shot or not. You run along tomorrow to the I.S.C., like the fine Millington girl I know you are. I'll come over there and visit you sometime this week. Mr. Pugh assures me that it's a first-rate rehabilitational facility."

Rehabilitational facility. Beth shuddered, but Mr. Stuart didn't seem to notice. He was still talking.

"I'll do what I can to straighten the rest of this mess out—you still have to see Dr. Dycus, don't you?"

"Tomorrow morning," Beth said.

Mr. Stuart nodded. "Well, you go ahead and do that. Why, you may not need any of my help at all." He punched the down button, and as they waited for a car he said, "But no more nonsense from your mother about a lawsuit, hear? You tell her for me that if she plays ball, I'll play ball." The bell dinged and the elevator door slid open. Beth stepped inside, and pressed "L" as Mr. Stuart called after her.

"One more thing. I don't want Jed worrying about any of this, do you understand? We'll just keep this conversation between us. That boy's got enough to worry about. If that leg don't heal right, he could lose his football scholarship."

The door slid closed. Beth didn't have to answer him.

FIFTEEN

Beth had seen Helen Dycus a few times when she had come to honors assemblies at Millington, but neither she nor her parents had ever been introduced. She regretted that now, as the three of them waited to be summoned into the superintendent's elaborate office. It would be nice to be able to say, "Hi. You remember me, don't you?" Beth looked at the clock on the wall. It said 10:10.

A buzzer sounded, and Dr. Dycus's secretary said, "You may go in now."

Helen Dycus was a woman in her early fifties. Before taking this job eighteen months ago, she had supervised the school at Glenhaven, a minimum security facility for young women who had had their first skirmish with the law. When she came to Fort Preston there had been a great deal of controversy over her stern, no-nonsense approach to public school education, but so far, she had managed to appear fair and reasonable. Most people seemed to like her.

After the introductions were over, Helen Dycus offered the O'Connors coffee, which all three of them declined. Dr. Dycus poured a cup for herself, smiled slightly, and settled into the leather chair behind her desk. "Who would like to begin?" she said, looking at Beth, who looked to her mother.

Joanne O'Connor began to explain the circumstances surrounding Beth's arrest—the failure to read her rights, the lack of a phone call.

As soon as Helen Dycus picked up on the direction of the conversation, she interrupted. "I find this irrelevant to our discussion, Mrs. O'Connor. As you know, the school district has dropped the criminal charges."

"They are the only ones you should have pursued," Joanne O'Connor said.

"I certainly can see about reinstating them, if that would make you happy." Helen Dycus's voice was oily. The comment—or was it a threat?—slipped out easily. Beth could feel panic hit her. She didn't want criminal charges on her record.

Joanne O'Connor remained calm. "If that's what you choose to do, we can air all of our grievances in court. They all deal with civil rights violations, anyway. But in view of the tragedy that happened Saturday night, I should think you would want to put this entire episode behind you as quickly as possible. You did realize the president of your school board started this entire thing by stealing that stupid plaster cougar, didn't you?"

"Mother!" Beth shouted.

"It's important that Dr. Dycus know this, Beth. She can't make a decision about your sentence to the I.S.C. if she doesn't have all the facts."

Helen Dycus's face remained immobile and she let her eyes flick from one O'Connor face to another without saying a word. Beth's mother saw that the superintendent was not going to comment, so she pressed on. "Jed Stuart has also told me that I cannot appeal any administrative decision to the school board. I find that totally incomprehensible."

"You have already had a hearing with Willard Pugh. Now you are appealing to me. The school board is far too busy to listen to each and every parental complaint." Helen Dycus drained her coffee cup and put her hands on the arms of her chair. Beth knew she was signaling the end of the interview, but Joanne O'Connor had come to speak her piece, and she was not going to be stopped.

"The hearing with Willard Pugh was a joke. Beth's suspension notice and transfer to the I.S.C. were already completed before we arrived. It's obvious. He'd backed himself into a corner with his public announcement of Beth's punishment, and he wasn't about to retreat."

"I don't think that's an accurate statement, Mrs. O'Connor," said the superintendent in an even tone of voice. "Willard Pugh listens carefully and makes his judgments accordingly. He reduced the punishment of John Bartlett, and Carl Loessing as well. I believe neither of them was sentenced to the I.S.C. So you see, Mr. Pugh wasn't backed into a corner at all." Helen Dycus turned in her chair. "Beth has admitted being at the school, and further, she's admitted painting the car. John and Carl both claim they were merely at Woodrow, but didn't do any vandalism. Under those circumstances Willard Pugh felt justified in reducing their sentences."

"He reduced their sentences because of that stupid football game, and you know it! Surely you don't think those boys were just innocent observers!" Franklin O'Connor burst out. "I think we have a case of sex discrimination here, too."

"What we think has nothing to do with it, Mr. O'Connor," the superintendent said. "The boys say they did nothing, and there is no evidence to prove otherwise. Are you asking me to trample on their civil rights?"

Joanne's hands were shaking and for a moment Beth wondered if her mother might be going to cry. Instead, Mrs. O'Connor stared steadily at the superintendent. "I've chatted with a lawyer and he tells me that something called 'notice' is a part of everyone's civil rights, Dr. Dycus. It's part of the due process protection that's guaranteed in the First Amendment. After all, we can't obey a law if we don't know what it is. I'm sure you're aware of this, coming from Glenhaven."

The superintendent pursed her lips at the mention of

her former job, but said nothing. Beth and her father exchanged glances. When had Joanne come up with this information? Beth's mother pulled the Millington High School student handbook out of her purse, opened it to the section on discipline and jurisdiction of the school, and handed the book to the superintendent, who glanced at it but avoided reading it.

Beth stole a glance at her mother, who now appeared relaxed and in control of the situation. She pressed on with her argument. "I had hoped to avoid appealing to technicalities and violations of policy, Dr. Dycus, but that handbook puts students on notice that the school can only use school punishment on them when they misbehave during the school day or at school-sponsored events. According to this handbook's definition of school jurisdiction, Beth was at Woodrow on her own time."

A flash of surprise crossed the superintendent's face, but it passed as quickly as it came. "Mrs. O'Connor, I think you'll find there's a policy in this book that covers Beth's assignment to the I.S.C. or any other kind of punishment Willard Pugh might have thought appropriate." Helen Dycus reached behind her and pulled a policy book, identical to the one Willard Pugh had in his office, off her credenza. She flipped through its pages until she came to the section she wanted, cleared her throat, and allowed a slight smile to play around her mouth. Beth felt a chill. Whatever the superintendent was going to read would not be good.

Helen Dycus had the book open to the section called "Dress Code," and she read aloud. "How students dress, talk, and behave at all times and at all places reflects on their individual schools and the school district as a whole. Consequently, the school district reserves the right to inflict disciplinary action for any violation of dress, behavior, or speech standards." As she read the words of this policy, Helen Dycus emphasized "at all times" and "at all places."

Joanne O'Connor's mouth dropped open. "Are you saying that Willard Pugh could punish Beth, or any of his students, for the kind of bathing suits they might wear to the beach on Saturday?"

"Well, I seriously doubt that Mr. Pugh would concern himself with things like that, but yes . . . technically, he could," the superintendent answered, snapping the book shut with a flourish. "There are some kinds of bathing suits that would not reflect well on their wearer and, consequently, on the person's school."

"My goodness. Maybe Mr. Pugh would like to move in and finish raising Ruthanne. Sometimes I don't like what she wears to church. And I had no idea that I could call on him to give her detentions when she doesn't clean up her room. After all, a messy child doesn't reflect well on Millington, either. Perhaps, if she doesn't place in the barrel racing contest in Simonton, he could suspend her from school for a few days. That will encourage her to work Dunney more vigorously." Sarcasm dripped from Joanne's voice.

Franklin O'Connor had remained silent, but now he said, "When Mrs. O'Connor and I enrolled Bethany and her sister in kindergarten, we did not give you people jurisdiction over those children twenty-four hours a day for the next thirteen years 'at all places and at all times' . . . that's preposterous. It's also in direct contradiction with the statement in the student handbook. Which notice are we on, Dr. Dycus—the student handbook or your policy book? How many parents in this district know the school is watching its students twenty-four hours a day, just like some Big Brother?"

"Ignorance of the law is no excuse," the superintendent said primly. Beth's heart sank. How many times had she heard that argument?

Mr. O'Connor turned to Beth and Joanne. "Come on, we're leaving. There's nothing more to say." All four people rose at once, and Mr. O'Connor put his hands on the elbows of his daughter and his wife and guided them out of the superintendent's office, past her secretary, who didn't look up from her typing, and out the double glass doors of the administration building.

Once in the car, Joanne O'Connor leaned her head back against the seat. "Well, that's that," she said. "We gave it the old college try, and we lost." They were heading back to the I.S.C. and she turned in her seat to look at Beth. "Do you think they'll give you zeros for the work you missed this morning?" she asked.

"It doesn't matter," Beth said dully. She thought of Sabrina—she'd laugh at her mother's concern over a few zeros. "Is that all you've got to worry about?" she'd probably say. "Geeze!"

Franklin O'Connor looked at his wife. "Do you

think it would do any good to ask Jed Stuart again about a hearing in front of the school board? After what happened to his son, maybe he's changed his mind about this football fever that attacks everyone."

"No way," Beth said bitterly. "He still wants Jed to play ball for Texas. He's just mad because Millington lost the championship. And he sure doesn't want any more talk about his taking the cougar."

The gates swung open and the O'Connors drove through. When Beth got out of the car, her mother said, "I still think we should take these hypocrites to court."

Everyone was at lunch when Beth arrived. Sabrina was eating a baggie full of Chee-tos and she pushed it toward Beth when she sat down. "Well, what happened?" she said.

"Nothing, I suppose." The full impact of this morning's meeting was beginning to hit Beth, and she really didn't want to talk, but Sabrina was insistent. "I told you about me. What's the matter? You too good to talk about yourself?"

Beth played with a Chee-to, rolling it around on the table. "Did your mother ever consider suing the school district over what's happened to you?"

The girl laughed out loud. "That's a good one! Sue the school district? For what?"

Beth felt foolish. "I don't know. Civil rights violations, maybe?"

"Geeze! Listen to you. Baby, don't you know? Kids don't have civil rights. At least not here." Sabrina shook her head and went on shoving Chee-tos into her mouth. "Me, I'm gonna serve my time and then I'll just see about going back to old Rickover. I got a birthday in seven months. I'll be sixteen then, and believe me, it's adios amigos. No more school, and they won't be able to do a thing about it."

"You're fifteen and still in junior high?" The minute Beth said it, she regretted it. Sabrina's face turned ugly. "Yeah. Want to make something out of it? I should have been in tenth, but I got left back, okay?"

"It's fine. I'm sorry. I didn't mean to make you mad. But it's terrible to quit school—don't do it, Sabrina. Things will change."

"Give me a break," Sabrina answered. She picked up the empty Chee-tos bag and threw it in the trash can.

The buzzer sounded and the students lined up as they had been taught. The proctor reluctantly put down her copy of *Hairdo Magic* and led them back to their cubicles.

By the time Beth got home that afternoon she had made up her mind. She wanted her family to sue the school district.

"You're going to do what?" Martha was aghast when Beth called her late that afternoon to explain what was going to happen. "I think you're crazy. Just serve out your time in the I.S.C. It's not that long . . . six weeks. Then you'll be back at Millington and we can forget all about this mess."

"That's what I'm afraid of," Beth answered. "I'm afraid everybody will forget."

"That ought to make you happy. I wouldn't want people remembering that I spent a night in jail." Martha's voice resumed that superior tone that made Beth's skin crawl. "If you're not careful, you won't have any friends left, Beth. Except me."

Beth let out a heavy sigh into the phone. "Don't you see, Martha? We're doing this for everybody at Millington. Nobody thinks kids have any rights."

There was silence on the other end of the line for a moment, then Martha spoke. "Did you hear what Pugh did to Larry DeMont today?"

"How would I have heard anything? I just got home."

"It's pretty scary," Martha said. "After we lost the game, and everything else that happened, a bunch of us left the dance early. We just wanted to sit around and mourn, so we went to Achilles Pizza. Larry was with us. He was hurting, in real pain, you know? He took some good hits from those Woodrow animals. Anyway, it was taking forever to get the pizza, and Larry went up to the girl at the counter and complained. She sassed something back at him and he wound up calling her a real bad name. I know it was rude, but we didn't think anything more about it. We ate our pizza and left. Well, it seems the manager at Achilles saw Larry's Millington letter jacket and called the school this morning to complain. Pugh calls Larry into his office this afternoon and gives him six weeks in the I.S.C.! Larry says he's going to call the American Civil Liberties Union. Can you believe it?"

"Easily," Beth said bitterly. "I don't think Larry

should have lost his temper like that, but tell him I'm sorry and I wish him luck, because he's going to need it. There's a dress code policy that none of us knows about, but it's written down. It says that what we say and even how we dress—get this—*all the time*—reflects on the school and so the school can punish us. Better not wear that string bikini at spring break. Pugh'll get you."

Martha drew in her breath. "I see what you're saying, kid, but you know what else they say."

"What?" Beth demanded.

"You can't fight city hall," Martha answered.

"We're sure going to give it a try," Beth said.

❧ *E P I L O G U E* ❧

The graduating seniors of Millington High School gathered in a knot at the back of the coliseum, waiting for their cue to process in.

"I can't believe we finally made it, O'Connor," Martha said, slapping her friend on the back. Schoolmates since kindergarten, they would be separated from now on. Martha was going to the University of Texas and Beth, whose class rank had dropped drastically after her time at the I.S.C., was going to a small college in west Texas where the entrance requirements were not too rigid. The two friends signaled "thumbs up" to each other and took their places in the processional line.

"Good luck, Babe," Jed said as he slid past her. He

still held three conversations at once and raised a fist in greeting to those who passed by. After Beth returned to Millington, he spoke when they ran into each other, but that was the extent of their contact. He limped slightly now, and the doctors said he would never play football—or any other sport—professionally.

Her mortarboard was slipping, and Beth reached up to repin it in a kind of daze. Could this year really be over? The strains of "Pomp and Circumstance" filled the air. It was time to go. Two by two, the seniors solemnly began the walk to their seats. All of them tried hard to look dignified, but most barely managed to suppress their smiles.

When everyone was seated, the choir began to sing an anthem that was set to the words of James Russell Lowell.

> *Once to every man and nation, Comes the moment to decide, In the strife of truth with falsehood, For the good or evil side; . . . And the choice goes by forever, Twixt that darkness and that light.*

Choices. Beth thought of the ones she had made in this past year. Some were good; some were not. Her day in court had been a choice that she didn't regret. But it had been just that—one day, shortened when the judge announced that he wasn't interested in hearing anything about stolen cougars, school district policies, or school punishments. Those matters were not to be resolved in the nation's court system, he had said. Nevertheless, Beth remembered his lively inter-est in hearing about any possible violation of her civil rights.

Though the cause of evil prosper, Yet 'tis truth alone is strong;

Beth saw Willard Pugh lean over to say something to Helen Dycus. He looked peculiar in his academic gown, the familiar cowboy boots poking out from beneath its black folds. She remembered him on the witness stand, running his finger around his shirt collar as he testified. No, he had said. He had no recollection of announcing any punishments over the P.A. system of the school. No, he was certain that he had not filled out Beth's suspension form before he spoke to her. He had come to the decision to suspend her reluctantly after carefully weighing all the evi-dence.

Beth sighed and looked at Helen Dycus. The jewel-like colors in her doctoral hood gleamed against the black background of her robe. Her mortarboard was set squarely on top of her head and she was staring at the sea of faces in front of her. She looked every inch the superintendent of schools. She had been equally as imposing during the lawsuit, when she testified that Beth had had appeals to Willard Pugh and herself and that neither she nor Mr. Pugh had heard anything in those appeals that made them want to change her punishment. And no, the school board was under no obligation to hear any further appeals on Beth's behalf by her mother—or anyone else. "In my opinion this district has been more than fair," she had said.

Beth remembered waiting for the judge's decision in the courthouse coffee shop. She was surprised that she wasn't more nervous than she was. Instead, she'd felt empty inside, the way she did when Christmas Day, with all its weeks of frantic preparations, was finally drawing to a close. The empty feeling stayed with her when they reentered the courtroom to hear the judge's decision, and it remained with her for weeks afterward. The O'Connors lost the lawsuit, and Beth served out her full time in the I.S.C.

Though her portion be the scaffold, And upon the throne be wrong:

Beth looked at the dais where the diplomas were stacked. Jed Stuart, Sr., sat there with the entire school board. All were smiling broadly, happy that another graduating class was out of the way. Mr. Stuart didn't know it yet, but her mother was going to run against him in next year's school board election. The O'Connors' lawyer had talked Joanne into it while they waited for the judge's decision. "It doesn't matter how the judge rules in our case. It's just one case. If you don't like the way Jed Stuart and his crowd run this school district, find some good people—like yourself—and run against them. That's how to change things."

Beth thought of those who were missing from this ceremony, from school itself. Change would come too

184

late for them. Carl was going to graduate, but not from Millington. His parents had sent him to a private school near Dallas. Beth thought briefly of Sabrina and wondered what decision she had made about remaining in school.

Yet that scaffold sways the future, And, behind the dim unknown, Standeth God within the shadow, Keeping watch above his own.

The music swelled and hung in the air. Beth looked into the stands and saw Ruthanne waving wildly. She managed a conservative wave in return, one she hoped was in keeping with the dignity of the occasion. The lawsuit had been expensive, but Ruthanne had managed to hang onto Dunney. She had taken a job at Baskin-Robbins to help pay for his feed.

Franklin O'Connor aimed his camera at Beth and the flash went off. He smiled and made a circle with his thumb and forefinger. Beth smiled in return. Although several Texas banks had closed, Franklin O'Connor still had his job, and the bank's foreclosures were slowing down.

Joanne O'Connor, beautiful in a turquoise silk dress, blew Beth a kiss. Martha's parents were sitting with the O'Connors and they waved at Beth and blew kisses, too. Since Mr. Pugh refused to release a figure on the damages Beth might have done to the vocational ed car—"Because it didn't cost over twenty dollars to fix," Franklin O'Connor said—Martha and her parents insisted Joanne use the money Martha had collected as a start on her campaign fund. All of the contributors (whose names Martha still refused to reveal) agreed. Martha's father even offered to be Joanne's campaign manager, but Franklin O'Connor took that job himself. "We started this together, and the O'Connor family is going to finish it together," he had said. "I'll be campaign manager and Ruthanne and Beth will be chief envelope stuffers. Get the word out. We'll need volunteers. Change in this school district is on the way."

The senior class of Millington High School was ready to graduate, and everyone in the coliseum rose for the invocation. The words of the anthem echoed in Beth's head and she smiled, knowing in her heart that they were true.